The Forbidden Doors Series

FORBIDDEN ● DOORS

the curse

JAMES RIORDAN

Based on the Forbidden Doors series created by Bill Myers

 Tyndale House Publishers, Inc.   Wheaton, Illinois

Visit the exciting Web site for kids at www.cool2read.com
and the Forbidden Doors Web site at
www.forbiddendoors.com

Designed by Julie Chen

Published in association with the literary agency of Alive
Communications, Inc., 7680 Goddard Street., Suite 200,
Colorado Springs, CO 80920.

Scripture quotations are taken from the *Holy Bible,* New
Living Translation, copyright © 1996. Used by permission
of Tyndale House Publishers, Inc., Wheaton, Illinois 60189.
All rights reserved.

ISBN 0-8423-5739-4, mass paper

Printed in the United States of America

08 07 06 05 04 03 02
 7   6   5   4   3   2   1

*For my daughter,
Elicia, who gives me
such joy.*

Listen to me! You can pray for anything, and if you believe, you will have it.

Mark 11:24

1

here was an omi-
nous clunk under the Boeing 737. Rebecca
Williams stiffened, then glanced nervously at
her younger brother, Scott. He sat on her left
next to the window. Although he was her "little" brother, he would pass her in height
before long. He had a thin frame like
Becka's.

"It's just the landing gear coming down," he said, doing his best to sound like an experienced air traveler.

Becka nodded. She took a deep breath and tried to release her sweaty grip on the armrests. It didn't work. She didn't like flying. Not at all. Come to think of it, Becka didn't like the whole purpose of this trip.

Who did Z, the mysterious adviser on the Internet, think she was, anyway? What was he doing sending her and her brother off to Louisiana to help some girl caught up in voodoo? Granted, they'd had lots of experience battling the supernatural lately. First, there was the Ouija board incident at the Ascension Bookshop. Becka could never forget how Scott battled that group of satanists! They wanted revenge after Becka exposed Maxwell Hunter, the reincarnation guru. And let's not forget the so-called ghost at Hawthorne mansion, the counterfeit angel, and that last encounter with a phony UFO.

But voodoo in Louisiana? Becka didn't know a thing about voodoo. She barely knew anything about Louisiana.

Fortunately Mom had an aunt who lived in the area, so she'd insisted on coming along with them to visit her. Becka looked forward to seeing her great-aunt once more.

Becka looked to her right, where her mother rested comfortably, her eyes closed. *Good ol' Mom.* Maybe the trip would do her some good. Ever since Dad died she'd been fretting and working nonstop. This trip just might give her the rest she needed.

Clunk . . . clunk . . . brang!

Then again . . .

It was the same sound, only louder. Becka looked to Scott, hoping for more reassurance. "What's that clunking?" she asked.

Scott shrugged. "I don't know, but it's the *brang* that bothers me."

So much for reassurance.

Suddenly the intercom came on. "Ladies and gentlemen, this is your captain speaking. There seems to be a problem with the landing gear. . . ."

The collective gasp from the passengers did little to help Becka relax.

"I've radioed ahead for emergency measures. . . ."

Becka felt her mother's hand rest on top of hers. She turned to Mom.

"Don't worry," Mom said. "We'll be all right."

Don't worry?! Yeah, right.

The pilot's voice resumed. "The ground crew is going to spray the runway with foam."

3

"Foam?" Scott exclaimed. "Does he mean like shaving cream?"

"I'll advise you as the situation develops," the pilot continued. "Please try to remain calm."

CLUNK-CLUNK-BRAAANG!

The sound had grown steadily louder.

Becka looked past Scott out the window. They were flying low over New Orleans and dropping fast. As the plane suddenly banked to the left, she saw the airport and immediately wished she hadn't. Several large tankers sprayed foam on the runway. Fire trucks and ambulances were everywhere.

Now it was the head flight attendant's turn to be on the intercom. "Please make sure your seat belts are fastened securely across your lap. Then bend over as far as you can in the seat, keeping your head down. Hold a pillow to your face with one hand, and wrap your other arm around your knees."

Becka fought the fear down as she glanced at her mother. Mom had her eyes shut. Becka wondered if she was praying. Not a bad idea.

CLUNK-CLUNK-BRAAANG!

Another attendant hurried through the aisle, passing out pillows. She tried to appear calm but failed miserably.

The plane banked back to the right. Becka

laid her face down on the pillow in her lap and gave her seat belt another tug.

The intercom buzzed once more with the pilot's voice. "Ladies and gentlemen, we are about to land on the foam. . . . Please hold on."

CLUNK-CLUNK-BRAAANG!

"Don't be alarmed," he said. "That's just the landing gear. . . . I'll keep trying it as we come in."

Becka remained hunched over with her face on the pillow. She could feel the plane dropping, and still the landing gear was not coming down. They were going to land with no wheels!

CLUNK-CLUNK-BRAAANG!
CLUNK-CLUNK-BRAAANG!

She glanced at Scott, who stared back at her from his pillow. He tried to force an encouraging grin, but there was no missing the look of concern on his face.

She turned to look at Mom. Her eyes were still closed. Becka hoped that she continued to pray.

CLUNK-CLUNK-BRAAANG!
CLUNK-CLUNK-BRAAANG!

Becka's thoughts shot to Ryan Riordan, her boyfriend back home. If she died, how would he handle the news? And what about her friends—Julie, Krissi, and Philip? How would they handle it? She also thought of Dad—of perhaps seeing him soon. Too soon. It was this final thought that jolted her back to the present and caused her to pray. It wasn't that she didn't want to see Dad again. She just had a few more things to do first.

CLUNK-CLUNK-BRAAANG!
CLUNK-CLUNK-BRAAANG!!
CLUNK-CLUNK-CLUNK-
DAARRRRREEEEEEEE . . .

Something was different!

The plane veered sharply upward. Becka couldn't resist the temptation to sit up and glance out the window.

The pilot spoke once more. "Ladies and gentlemen, the landing gear has engaged. We are out of danger. I repeat. We are out of danger. We will land on a different runway in just a few moments."

"Thank you, Lord," Mom whispered. She sounded relieved as she sat up, then reached over and hugged both of her children. "Thank you . . ."

Becka breathed a sigh of relief as she joined the applause of the other passengers. They were safe. At least for now. But all the same, she couldn't help wondering if this was some sort of omen—a warning of the dangers that were about to begin.

The three o'clock bell at Sorrento High rang. Throngs of kids poured out of the old, weathered building. One fifteen-year-old girl slowed her pace as she headed for the bus. No one talked to her. Her clothes were more ragged than most. They were too shabby to be fashionable and too conservative to be alternative.

Sara Thomas had never fit in. She had never felt like she belonged, no matter where she was. As she approached the school bus and stepped inside, she steeled herself, waiting for the taunts.

None came. Just the usual after-school chatter.

Carefully she took a seat, stealing a glance to the rear of the bus. Ronnie Fitzgerald and John Noey were engrossed in a tattoo magazine.

Maybe they'd forget about her today.

With a swoosh and a thud, the door closed. The bus jerked forward.

Maybe today would be different.

Then again, maybe not. They had traveled less than a mile when it began. . . .

"Hey, Rags, you shopping at Goodwill or the Salvation Army these days?"

Sara recognized Ronnie's shrill, nasal voice.

"Hey! I'm talking to you."

She didn't turn around.

"I heard Goodwill's got a special on those cruddy, stained sweaters you like so much," John Noey said snidely.

Before she could catch herself, Sara glanced down at the brown chocolate stain on her yellow sweater.

The boys roared.

"Is that from a candy bar or did your dog do a number on it?" Ronnie shouted.

Most of the others on the bus smirked and snickered. A few laughed out loud.

Sara stared out the window as the taunts continued. As always, she tried to block out the voices. And, as always, she failed. But not for long.

Soon, she thought. *Soon they'll pay. They'll both pay.*

She reached into her purse and clutched the tiny cloth-and-straw doll. Already she was thinking about her revenge.

And already she was starting to smile.

~

Aunt Myrna's farmhouse was simple but clean. The furniture inside was made mostly of dark wood. The chairs looked like they'd been there a hundred years . . . and could easily last another hundred.

After Becka dropped her bags off in the small attic room that she would be using, she headed down to the kitchen, grabbed an apple out of the fruit basket, and strolled out to the front porch. As the screen door slammed, she vaguely heard Aunt Myrna telling Mom something about a farmhand named John Garrett who was supposed to drop by.

It was hot and humid, which reminded her of her childhood days in South America. Several months had passed since Dad's death and their move from Brazil back to California. But the humidity and the smells of the rich vegetation here in Louisiana sent her mind drifting back to the Brazilian rain forests.

Unlike California, everything in Louisiana was lush and wild. Plant life seemed to explode all around. And the water. There was water everywhere—lakes, ponds, and marshes. Although most of the area around the bayou was swamp, even the dry land never really felt dry. Still, it was beautiful.

Even surrounded by beauty, Becka felt nervous. Very nervous. Z had given them so little information. Just that a young girl named Sara Thomas lived in the area and that she was in serious trouble—caught up in some kind of voodoo. Z had also stressed that Becka and Scott were not to be afraid.

"Your training is complete," he had said. "Go in his authority."

His authority. God's authority. Becka had certainly seen God work in the past. There was no denying that. But even now as she looked around, she felt a strange sense of— what? Apprehension? Uncertainty?

During the other adventures, she had always been on her home turf. But being in a strange place, helping somebody she didn't even know . . . it all made her nervous. Very nervous.

The late afternoon sun shimmered on the vast sea of sugarcane before her as she sat on the steps. Wind quietly rippled through the cane, making the stalks appear like great scarecrows with arms beckoning her to come closer. Closer. Closer . . .

Something grabbed her hand.

Becka let out a gasp and turned to see a small goat eight inches from her face. It gobbled the last of her apple.

"Aunt Myrna!" she shrieked. "There's an animal loose out here!"

"He won't bother you none."

Becka turned, startled at hearing a voice come from the field of sugarcane. She tried to locate the source of the voice while keeping one eye on the goat in case he decided to go for a finger or two.

A young African-American man suddenly walked out of the field. Becka guessed that he was about seventeen. He was tall, lean, and handsome, in a rugged sort of way.

He nodded to the goat. "That's Lukey. He's more pet than farm animal." He entered the yard and stuffed his hands into his pockets. "Try scratching his nose. He likes that."

"Oh, that's OK," Rebecca said quickly. "I'd rather not just now." Then, rising to her feet, she said, "You must be John Garrett. Aunt Myrna said you'd be coming."

The young man nodded. "Miss Myrna said I should be showing you and your brother around the place some."

"So let's get started," Scott said, appearing suddenly in the doorway. "Wow. Cool goat. C'mere, boy." He crossed to the animal. It rubbed its head against his arm. "Hey!" Scott looked up with a broad smile. "He likes me!"

"He likes everybody," John Garrett said, already turning back toward the field. "We better get started if we're going. The foreman's called a meeting of us farmhands. It should be starting pretty soon."

Scott went to walk beside John. Becka fell in behind.

In seconds the two boys were hitting it off. Becka could only marvel. Her brother got along with everybody. In fact, when they'd moved to California, he fit in like he'd always been there. Unfortunately, it wasn't so easy for Becka to make friends. She figured that was partly why she felt so uncomfortable about this trip. She didn't like the idea of barging into a total stranger's life, even if they were supposed to help her.

But that was only part of the reason. There was something else: a feeling. It felt eerie . . . like something she couldn't quite explain but couldn't shake off.

"John," she called, trying to sound casual, "do you know anything about voodoo?"

He glanced back at her and laughed. "Not much. 'Cept my grandpa used to speak Gumbo all the time."

"Gumbo?" she asked.

"It's kind of a mesh of African dialects. A lot of the people into voodoo speak it. But you really got to be careful who you talk to about voodoo around these parts."

"Why's that?" Scott asked.

"Lots of folks believe in it, and if you upset them, they'd just as soon drop a curse on you as look at you."

Becka felt a tiny shiver run across her back. "A curse? Does stuff like that really happen?"

"Oh yeah. I heard about this woman who lived down the road from my father. She made an old *mambo* mad, and the *mambo* put a curse on her."

"Mambo?" Scott echoed with a snort. "Sounds like some kind of dance step."

John shot him a knowing look. "They're like high priestesses. And they're nothing to mess with."

"So what happened to this woman?" Scott asked.

"I heard she suddenly died in horrible pain."

"That's awful!" Becka shuddered. "Did you ever see her?"

John shook his head. "My father's cousin said he did, though. Not only that, I also heard about an old man who refused to pay the *hungan* for helping him get back his wife." At Scott's raised eyebrows John explained. "A *hungan* is like the male version of a *mambo*—the high priest. The man who wouldn't pay carried a powerful root with him at all times so the *hungan* couldn't work magic on him while he was alive. The root was like a good-luck charm. But when he died and they took him to the morgue, his body started shaking all over the place. And when they cut him open, they found he was full of scorpions!"

"Come on—scorpions?" Scott scoffed.

But Becka was not scoffing. In fact she felt

more uneasy by the moment. "How about him?" she asked. "Did you see him?"

John shook his head again. "No, that happened before I was born. I know it sounds crazy, but some of this curse stuff might be true."

Scott shook his head, his face filled with skepticism. "I don't know. Sounds pretty fantastic to me. Like something out of a B movie."

"Maybe so," John continued. "But one thing I do know, and that's to never cross Big Sweet. I've heard his magic's powerful."

"Who's Big Sweet?" Scott asked.

"You don't know who Big Sweet is? He's Miss Myrna's foreman. He's head of the harvest crew. Been picking sugarcane all his life. That's why they call him Big Sweet."

"Why's he so dangerous?" Becka asked.

"He's the local *hungan*. People say his father was a disciple of Marie Leveau. She's called the Queen of Conjure. She was a powerful *mambo* who used to live in the French Quarter of New Orleans."

"And you're afraid of him?" Becka asked.

"Everybody's afraid of Big Sweet." John turned back to Becka. There was something about his look that caused a cold knot to form deep in her stomach. "Everybody's afraid . . . and you'd better be, too."

Suddenly a horn bellowed across the fields. John spun toward the sound, looking startled.

"What's that?" Scott asked.

The other boy started moving away from them toward the sound. Becka and Scott exchanged concerned glances. John was clearly very nervous. "That's Big Sweet's horn," he said. "It's his conch shell. The meeting's starting. I gotta go."

"What about showing us the farm?" Scott called as John moved away.

"I can take you into the swamp tomorrow after chores. But I gotta go now."

"Yeah, but—"

"Look, I can't be late. I gotta go." With that he disappeared into the cane.

"John!" Scott called. "Hey, John! Hold on a minute!"

But there was no answer.

Scott turned to Becka. She knew her expression held the same concern she saw in her brother's face. The horn continued to bellow. Finally Becka cleared her throat. "I . . . uh . . . I guess we'd better head back."

"Yeah. I can't wait to get the lowdown on all this stuff from Z tonight. I'll bet he knows about this Big Sweet guy."

"And Sara Thomas," Becka reminded him.

"Right," Scott said. "But the more we learn

about Big Sweet, the faster we'll be able to blow him away."

"Blow him away?" Becka felt herself growing impatient with her brother. "Come on, Scotty. You sound like a Schwarzenegger movie."

"That's me!" Scott threw a few mock karate kicks. "Scott Williams, Demon Terminator."

"Scott, this isn't a joke."

"What's the matter? Afraid Big Sweet may slap a curse on you?"

"Stop it!"

"Afraid he might hatch a lizard in your ear or give you a monkey face? Hmmm, looks like somebody's already done that."

"Scotty!"

"Come on, Beck—lighten up!" Then, looking across the field, his face lit up with an idea. "Let's save ourselves a little time and take a shortcut through the cane."

Becka began to protest, but her brother had already started out. And there was one thing about Scott—when he made up his mind to do something, there was no stopping him. With a heavy sigh, she followed.

The stalks of cane towered over their heads. Becka knew that Scott was right about one thing. By taking this shortcut they'd get back to the house a lot faster. And with all the uneasiness she had been feeling out there, especially now that they were alone . . . well, the sooner they got home, the better.

Unfortunately, "sooner" was way too long, now that Scott was in his teasing mode. He kept jumping around and darting between the stalks of cane like some ghoul.

Brothers. What a pain, Becka thought.

"Oogity-boogity! Me Big Sweet. Me cast a big curse on you."

"Knock it off!" Becka muttered between clenched teeth. She was going to bean him if he kept it up.

"Big Sweet turn you into little mouse if you're not careful."

"Scott, you know you're not supposed to joke around with—"

"Oogity-boogity!" He leaped even higher into the air.

"Scotty . . ."

"Oogity-boogity! Oogity-boog—OW!"

Suddenly he crumpled to the ground.

Becka's heart pounded as she raced to his side. "What happened? Are you OK?"

"I twisted my ankle!" he whined. "Owwww!"

Becka knew it served him right. But since he was clearly in pain, now was not the time to bring it up. Instead, she reached out and carefully touched his ankle.

"Ouch!" he yelped. "That hurts!"

"Sorry. Here . . ." She tried to help him to

his feet. "Lean against me and see if you can—"

"Oww!" he cried even louder. "I can't. It hurts too much. You'll have to get somebody to—"

Suddenly there was a low, distant growl. It sounded part animal and part . . . well, Becka couldn't tell. It was mixed with another sound—a silent, whooshing noise.

"What's that?" Scott said, his eyes wide and suddenly alarmed.

Becka wished she had a good answer. She didn't. "I—I don't know." She rose to her feet and searched the field. "I can't see anything but sugarcane."

The sound grew louder. Becka felt her pulse kick into high gear. Whatever it was, it was moving. And by the sound of things, it was moving toward them.

Once again, Scott tried to stand, but it was no use. As soon as he put any weight on his ankle, it gave out. He toppled back to the ground.

The noise grew closer.

"Becka . . ." There was no missing the fear in her brother's voice.

Becka reached for him, fighting off the fear that swept over her. She had no idea what was coming at them, but she knew lying down, unable to move, was no way for her brother to meet it. She tried pulling him forward, but he was too heavy.

The cane several yards in front of them suddenly splintered.

"Becka!"

All at once something exploded through the stalks. It was big and red.

It headed directly for them.

"What is it?!" Scott cried.

"I don't know!"

"Becka!"

She reached under his arms, trying to pull him to the side, to get him out of the way.

And still the thing bore down on them, ripping cane just a few yards in front of them and devouring it with giant, red jaws.

"Run!" Scott shouted at her. "Get out of here!"

The afternoon sun caught a sharp, shiny blade coming directly toward them, slicing through cane only a few feet away.

"Get out of here!" Scott yelled at her.

She pulled harder, but it was no use.

"Beck—"

She finally looked up. The giant blade hovered over her and was coming down fast. She screamed and gave one last tug, moving her brother only a foot before tumbling backward. The blade came down.

"Your leg!" Becka screamed. "Your—"

Scott tucked and rolled just as the blade chomped down, missing his flesh by inches.

The threshing machine roared past them, leaving a great swath of cut sugarcane in its path.

Becka couldn't see the driver, but as the machine passed, she could read a name crudely painted on the back. It was in big black letters. Originally, it had read *BIG SWEET'S CANE KILLER.* But over the years dirt and grime had covered some of the letters. Now it read *BIG SWEET CAN KILL.*

2

$\mathcal{S}$ara sat in front
of the cracked dresser mirror. Carefully she
outlined her lips with dark lip liner before
applying a deep burgundy lipstick. So far,
she could have been any teenage girl applying any makeup.

So far.

Next she picked up a medium-sized paintbrush, dipped it in bloodred paint, and drew

a streak across her left cheek. She did the same with the right.

Then came the blue. Jagged lines, like small lightning bolts, painted above each eye.

And finally the green. This time she covered her entire chin and the lower part of her neck. At last Sara put down the brush and admired her handiwork. She was very pleased.

~

An hour after their encounter with the threshing machine, Scott sat in his great-aunt's best easy chair with his ankle packed in ice. He quietly watched a baseball game on television and poked at some potato chips on his plate.

Becka sat nearby thinking how strange it was for her brother to be so silent. Normally he'd be milking his injury for all it was worth, getting people to wait on him hand and foot. But he'd hardly said a word.

Even Mom noticed. When Becka entered the kitchen to get a refill on her lemonade, Mom said, "Why don't you talk to your brother? He seems so blue."

"What am I supposed to say?"

"It's not so much what you say," Mom replied. "It's your attitude. Just be there for him. You're a team now. If one of you is down, the other should try to help him up."

Becka shrugged, poured her lemonade, and strolled back into the living room. "So," she said, trying to sound casual, "it's almost nine. Think we should give Z a try?"

Scott glanced at his watch. "Yeah, I guess."

"Scotty?" She plopped down on the foot-rest directly between him and the TV. "What's wrong?"

"Hey, you're blocking my view. Move."

"Not until you tell me what's eating you."

"Becka . . ."

"Talk to me."

"Beck."

"I mean it."

He let out a sigh of exasperation.

"Is it the threshing machine with Big Sweet's name on it?"

He shook his head and glanced away. "That's only part of it." She continued to wait. After a moment, he continued. "I'm scared, Beck. This time I'm really nervous."

Becka bit her lip. It was one thing for her to be nervous. But Scott? As far as she knew, her little brother wasn't afraid of anything. Normally his faith in God gave him confidence. She'd never seen him look this discouraged.

"First, our plane almost crashes. *Then,* my ankle gets twisted. *Then,* we nearly get turned into hamburger by some crazed farm machinery. All this and we haven't even talked to the girl yet."

Becka swallowed and tried to keep her voice even. "So, you think they're all related?"

"Don't you?"

Becka slowly answered, "I think someone or something doesn't want us here—that's for sure. And I think whatever it is is very powerful."

Scott nodded in silent agreement.

For a long moment, neither said a word. Finally, Scott reached for the laptop computer he'd borrowed from a friend and turned it on. He'd already plugged it into Aunt Myrna's phone line. Now it was simply a matter of connecting with Z in an Internet chat room.

Neither of them knew who Z was or why he had taken such an interest in them. They didn't understand how he could know so many little things about their lives—personal things that no one else would know. Then there was his knowledge about the occult. On more than one occasion he had gotten them out of jams with knowledge only some kind of expert would have.

Of course they'd tried to track Z down to find out who he was. But each time they tried, Z foiled their attempts somehow. Whoever this Z was, he was very clever—and very, very secretive.

"Cool," Scott said as he stared at the screen. "Z's online, waiting for us."

Becka moved in closer to look.

Good evening, Scott, Rebecca. Sorry about the scare on the airplane.

Becka fought off a shudder. It was just that type of knowledge that unnerved her about Z.

Scott was already typing his comeback:

How did you know about the plane?

Z didn't answer his question. But that was no big surprise. He never explained how he knew what he knew. Instead, other words began to form on the screen.

Before you contact Sara Thomas, you should be aware of the facts on voodoo.

Scott and Becka threw each other a glance. It was typical of Z to get right to the heart of the matter.

Like many superstitions, much of voodoo's power comes from the belief people have

about it. Often too much credit is given to it. it is
blamed for every bad thing that happens.

Scott typed back:

Are you telling us it's all just superstition?

Z's response came quickly:

Not always. In many cases demonic activity can
feed off the fear and superstition voodoo
engenders. Regardless, it is important
to remember that as Christians, the only
power voodoo—or any evil—holds over you is
the power you give it because of your fear.
Do not forget this.

Becka stared at the screen as Scott began
typing another question:

Where did voodoo come from?

Voodoo is a combination of West African
traditions and rituals from Catholic missionaries.
The term comes from the West African word
vodun and the creole French word *vaudau*, both of
which mean "spirit." Ceremonies consist of
singing, drumming, and praying to the dead,
whom they call the *loa*.

Becka leaned over her brother. "Ask about Sara. Where is she? How do we find her?"

But before Scott could type the words, Z answered the question:

Sara Thomas works at the Sorrento library on Saturdays. Contact her there. It is a twenty-minute bus ride from your great-aunt's house. Remember, people usually become part of voodoo to try to get control of their life. They use black magic and curses to seek protection from the supernatural or to get power over others. They are usually more deluded than evil. But that doesn't mean they aren't dangerous. Be careful. Good night.

Scott immediately began typing:

Wait. Don't go yet. We need to know more.

At first they thought he'd logged off. But after a moment, the final comment appeared:

I must go. You've been trained. You have the Word, and you have your Lord. The only power voodoo has over you is the power you give it through your fear. Your tools are prayer and faith. If you remember these, you will be victorious. Should trouble arise, seek help from the local pastor. Good-bye. Z

"Good-bye?!" Scott turned to his sister in panic. "What does he mean 'good-bye'?"

"I guess—" Becka took a deep breath— "I guess he means we're on our own."

Scott spun back to the computer. "No way! Not this time! Not here!"

Z . . . Z, are you there? Z, answer me. . . .

The two waited silently for an answer. But there was none. Z had left the chat room.

"Great!" Scott said. "Just great! He sends us all the way out here, then just leaves us on our own!" He angrily snapped off the computer.

Becka ventured a thought. "If Z says we can do it, then maybe—"

"We can't do this!" Scott interrupted. "Not on our own! You know what we've been through. We haven't even met this . . . this Sara chick. We're going to need some help. Lots of it."

Becka agreed. "He said if we get into trouble we should contact a local pastor."

"A local pastor?" Scott repeated. "What local pastor? We're out here in the middle of Hicksville! What would any pastor out here know?"

"Excuse me?" It was Aunt Myrna poking her head in from the kitchen. "Did you kids say you were looking for a pastor?"

Scott and Becka exchanged glances.

"I go to the church over in Sorrento. Maybe you'd like to meet my pastor? Our church is the little one right next to a park."

"Uh, yeah, well . . . thanks, Aunt Myrna," Scott said, doing his best to sound polite. "We'll sure give that some thought."

"That would be nice. I'm sure Pastor Barchett would be able to help you," she said with a smile as she disappeared back into the kitchen.

"Sorrento?" Becka repeated. "Did she say 'Sorrento'?"

"Yeah . . ."

"Isn't that where Z—"

Scott finished the sentence, "—said Sara was working."

The two traded nervous looks. Was it just coincidence, or had the mysterious Z given them more information than they'd thought?

"We'll try again tomorrow night," Scott ventured. "Maybe he'll be back online."

Becka nodded, but she had her doubts. Even now she suspected this encounter was going to be different from the others. Different and far more dangerous.

~

In the darkness, the drums pounded.

Doomba-doomba-doom. Doomba-doomba-doom.

Sara pushed her way through the branches toward the sound. For the hundredth time she wondered if she should go back home. She had a nagging feeling that this was wrong. Very wrong. But each time she thought of turning back, she remembered Ronnie Fitzgerald and John Noey. Their voices, their merciless taunts. No. It had been going on too long. It was time to stop it.

Now.

Doomba-doomba-doom. Doomba-doomba-doom.

The drums grew louder. She was getting closer.

Sara had been to voodoo ceremonies before, but only the public ones—never the secret rites. These secret ceremonies were held in secluded places and known only to members of the cult . . . and to those about to be initiated.

That last phrase stuck in her mind. *Those about to be initiated.* Sara felt her heart beating harder, almost in rhythm with the drums.

Doomba-doomba-doom. Doomba-doomba-doom.

Through the leaves, she could see the glimmer of a fire. She had found them. They had not given her directions—just simply told her to follow the sound of the drums.

Doomba-doomba-doom. Doomba-doomba-doom.

She forced herself to go forward, her legs weak and trembling with fear. She knew the stories. She knew what voodoo could do to you. But she also knew what it could do *for* you. How it could protect you from the others, from the Ronnie Fitzgeralds and John Noeys of the world.

She continued through the brush.

Now she was close enough to see the people dancing about the fire. Some moved in perfect rhythm to the drums. Others darted about, convulsing and writhing like wild animals.

She reached the edge of the clearing. This was her last chance to turn back.

She took a deep, unsteady breath, clutched the small cloth doll hanging around her neck, and entered the clearing.

∾

"Scott. Scotty, wake up!"

It was his sister's voice, but it sounded like it was coming from a long, long way away.

"Scotty, you're dreaming! Scotty, wake up!"

Suddenly he bolted upright. It took a moment to get his bearings, to realize he'd fallen asleep in the hammock on the porch.

"You OK?" Becka asked. "It sounded like you were having a nightmare."

Scott frowned, trying hard to remember. "Yeah . . . I don't . . . I think I heard screaming. In my dream, someone or something was screaming and—"

Doomba-doomba-doom.

He froze. "What's that?"

Doomba-doomba-doom. Doomba-doomba-doom.

The screen door creaked loudly. Aunt Myrna stepped onto the porch carrying two glasses of lemonade. "You kids want a cold drink?"

"Aunt Myrna, what's that noise?" Scott asked.

She paused to listen. "Oh," she said, handing out the glasses. "It's them."

"Them?" Becka asked.

"Yes. Big Sweet and his group. They have a voodoo ceremony most every night this time of year." She gave a gesture of distaste. "You'll get used to the drums after a while."

Scott and Becka exchanged glances, both knowing that they would never get used to it.

"Oh, Rebecca?" Aunt Myrna stood at the door, ready to go in. "Did Lukey—you know, my goat—did he follow you out into the cane fields today?"

"No, I don't think so," Becka answered. "Why?"

"Oh, no reason," Aunt Myrna said, running her hands through her hair. It was long and gray and beautiful. "It's just . . . well, I guess he's run off again. Can't seem to find him anywhere. Well—" she forced a smile and headed back into the house—"I'm sure he'll turn up."

The door slammed shut behind her, but Scott barely noticed. He was feeling very sick.

"Scotty, what's wrong?" Becka asked. "Are you OK?"

He nodded. When he spoke, his voice was strangely hoarse. "The screaming . . . in my dream . . ."

"Yeah . . ."

The drums grew louder now.

Doomba-doomba-doom. Doomba-doomba-doom.

"What about it?" Rebecca asked.

"It definitely wasn't a person or anything like that. I remember now. It was an animal."

"An animal?"

Scott nodded. "And it wasn't screaming— it was bleating . . . 'cause it was being slaughtered."

"Bleating?" Becka repeated.

"Yeah, you know . . . like a goat."

The great conch horn sounded, sending its haunting echo throughout the woods.

3

The morning air
was so fresh and beautiful that Becka almost
forgot their purpose, let alone the danger
that surrounded them.

Almost.

The weather forecast promised that rain
would move in later that day, but for now
everything smelled warm and moist and full

of life. Becka especially loved the flowers. They were her passion, her weakness. They always had been. And as she and Scott headed down Aunt Myrna's long driveway to the main road, a gentle breeze stirred and brought half a dozen different fragrances to her.

Scott's ankle was much better. He limped only slightly as they approached the mailbox and began the wait for the bus to Sorrento.

Unfortunately, when the old, broken-down vehicle finally appeared, it belched out more smoke than Mom had created the last time she tried to barbecue. The metal beast screeched to a halt before them. As they boarded and headed to the back, any fragrance of flowers was blotted out by the smell of diesel oil and exhaust fumes.

The gears ground loudly as the bus lumbered down the road. Soon they passed a large potato field, then a group of run-down shacks. Dirty-faced children in ragged clothes ran all around the yards.

"Look how they're dressed," Becka said sadly.

Scott nodded. "And check out their shoes."

Becka looked. "They don't have any."

"Exactly."

Becka nodded. "I read that voodoo is most widespread among the poor. Like Z said, it's a way for them to try to gain some control over their lives."

Scott grunted. "Doesn't look like it's working too well."

Becka watched a young mother rushing to pick up a dirt-smeared child who had fallen near the ditch. The little one didn't appear hurt, but the mother carefully soothed and cuddled him, tenderly holding him in her arms. Becka sighed, touched by the love the mother had for her child, yet sad at the same time. "It's terrible what happens to people who don't have a lot of hope."

Scott nodded.

Suddenly there was a loud explosion.

"What was that?!" Becka cried.

"A blown tire," Scott guessed. He grabbed the seat in front of him and held on.

Had the bus been a newer model, it might have held on to the road. Being old and decrepit, the bus went into a tailspin. The back end—where Becka and Scott sat—skidded toward the oncoming traffic.

The two looked out of their window just as the bus hurtled toward a tractor. The tractor driver turned hard. But the bus kept going at it, brakes screeching as the tires smoldered from the friction with the road.

At last they skidded to a stop only a few

feet from the tractor. But the trouble wasn't over yet. The bus started tipping. Becka let out a scream, certain they were going over. Suddenly it stopped and righted itself with a mighty thud.

"Sorry 'bout that folks!" the driver called back. "Everyone OK?"

Other than arriving in Sorrento an hour and a half late (it took the bus driver that long to find his tools and fix the tire), Becka and Scott were fine. Well, not exactly fine. Narrowly escaping a plane crash, nearly being chopped by a thresher, and now surviving a bus accident—all within the first twenty-four hours of their arrival—had taken its toll.

"That does it!" Scott said as he stormed off the bus and over to a small park. "I'm not going anywhere the rest of the time we're here!"

"Scotty."

"Say what you want, Beck! Something's after us. Somebody's definitely put some sort of curse on us!"

Becka took a moment to quiet her own fears, then tried to explain. "Remember what Z said? Even if it is a curse, even if it is real, the only power it has over us is fear. We have to trust that God—"

But Scott was in no mood to listen to reason. "I think we should turn right around and go back to California."

She knew he had a point. Something *was* definitely going on. If whoever—or *whatever*—it was wanted to scare them, it was doing a pretty good job. Still, Z had never been wrong before.

She looked up to see Scott heading across the road. "Hey!" she called. "Where are you going?"

Scott pointed to the large building directly in front of them. "Z said this Sara babe worked at the library, right?" He motioned ahead of him. "Well, there's the library."

Becka crossed the road and joined him. "Listen," she said as they headed up the steps, "better let me do the talking." It wasn't that she wanted to be the one who spoke to Sara. Far from it. She just knew from experience that Scott was in no mood to be overly sensitive—which meant he'd probably offend everyone in his path.

They opened the library door and stepped in. Becka led the way to the circulation desk, where an older woman checked out books. "Excuse me," Becka said, "we're looking for Sara Thomas. Is she here?"

The older woman smiled and nodded toward two young girls who were shelving books.

One girl looked fairly normal. The other one had wild hair with purple highlights. She wore a black leather jacket with small chains attached to the pockets.

Becka took a deep breath. "Well, here goes."

They walked across the room straight to the purple-haired girl.

"Can I help you?" the girl asked.

"Uh, yes," Rebecca began. "This is probably going to sound a little crazy to you, but a friend of ours on the Internet, whose name is Z, asked us to visit you to . . . to try to help you through some sort of voodoo thing."

The girl made a face. "Some sort of what?"

Becka tried again. "Your voodoo thing. We have some experience with the occult and . . ."

"Voodoo?" The girl looked at Becka like she had a screw loose. "My *voodoo thing?* What are you, some kind of wacko? I don't have any voodoo thing."

"But aren't you . . . aren't you Sara Thomas?"

The girl snorted and shook her head. "No. My name is Stacy. This is Sara Thomas."

With great embarrassment, Becka turned to face the other girl—the "normal"-looking one—who now glared at her.

"Nice job, Sis," Scott muttered quietly.

"I'm sorry," Becka stuttered. "I . . . I didn't mean . . ."

The purple-haired girl nodded and went back to shelving books.

Becka turned to Sara. "Hello." She smiled self-consciously. "You're Sara?"

Sara Thomas nodded. "Yes." Her voice was cold. "And you are?"

"I'm Rebecca Williams. This is my brother, Scott. We're here from California to—"

"Yes, I heard," Sara cut her off. "You're here to help me deal with my 'voodoo thing.'"

Becka tried to snicker, hoping that Sara would join in and they could laugh off the whole silly thing. But Sara wasn't laughing. She wasn't even smiling. Becka was forced to continue. "Yes, I'm sorry about that. . . . I, uh—"

"Listen," Sara cut her off again. "I don't know you. I don't even have a computer, so I certainly don't know anyone named Z. And what's more, I don't need your help. I don't *want* your help. And I think you'd better go now." That said, Sara turned her attention to her books.

Becka stood for a long moment staring at Sara's back, trying to think of something to say. Finally she cleared her throat. "Look, I'm very sorry. I didn't mean any harm."

Without turning to her, Sara said, "Would you just go, please?"

"Listen." Scott stepped forward. The tone of his voice was not happy. "We didn't come all the way to Louisiana just to—"

"Never mind," Becka interrupted quickly. "We've, uh, we've bothered her long enough. We should go."

"Yeah, but—"

"Let's go." She took Scott's arm and started turning him toward the door. It was only then that she caught sight of something that sent a chill through her. She hadn't noticed it before, but Sara was now fingering something hanging on a chain around her neck. A small cloth doll.

A doll that looked very similar to the ones the witch doctors used in Brazil.

~

They were halfway down the library steps when Scott let out an exasperated sigh. "So tell me, could we have messed that up any worse?"

"We just got off on the wrong foot," Becka answered. "That's all."

"Well, she doesn't want our help. I think she made that pretty clear."

Becka nodded and was about to speak when something else caught her eye. Across the road was the small park beside which was a small church. "Isn't that the church Aunt Myrna was talking about?"

Scott followed her gaze and shrugged. "I guess. She said it was next to a park."

Becka nodded and started for it.

"Becka . . ."

"Come on. We've got an hour before the bus leaves."

A reluctant Scott followed. Although he limped a bit more, he joined his sister anyway.

They knocked on the door of the church. The pastor was not there. Instead, an elderly lady answered and directed them to the parsonage next door.

They crossed to a small house. Becka noticed that part of the porch stairs had rotted. It had also been a long time since the building had seen a paintbrush. She knocked on the door, but there was no answer. She tried again with the same result. Then one final time.

There was no answer.

As they started back down the steps, the door suddenly opened. A small, frail, elderly man appeared. "May I help you?"

"Oh—" Becka turned. "We thought no one was home."

The older man smiled. "I'm home, but

I'm slow. It takes me a while to get to the door."

"We're looking for Pastor Barchett," Scott said.

The older man nodded. "That's me."

"My name is Rebecca Williams. This is my brother, Scott. We're here visiting Myrna Carmen. She's my mother's aunt."

Pastor Barchett looked confused. "Who?"

Scott shot a glance at Becka as if to say, "Here we go again."

"Myrna Carmen," Becka repeated. "She attends your church."

"She's been a member here for like a zillion years," Scott added.

"Oh . . . Myrna." The pastor broke into a grin. "My goodness, yes. So you're Myrna's . . . what did you say?"

"Great-niece and nephew," Becka said.

"Ah yes, of course."

"Anyway, we wondered if we could have a few moments of your time."

Pastor Barchett stepped back from the door and graciously waved them in. "Of course, of course."

Inside, the house was small and well kept . . . except for a cat box that needed to be changed.

Pretending not to notice the odor, Becka said, "What a nice house you have."

"One of the ladies from the church comes in every few days and cleans it," the pastor said as he closed the door. "All I have to do is pick up after myself and . . ." He trailed off, forgetting what the other thing was until he noticed Scott's upturned nose. "And change the cat litter, that's it! Sorry about the smell. I forget because the old nose ain't what she used to be. Would you two like some tea?"

Scott shook his head to Becka. She took the cue. "No thanks."

Pastor Barchett motioned for them to sit on the sofa. He took a seat across from them. "So . . . how can I help you?"

Becka leaned forward. "Pastor, do you know much about voodoo?"

"I should hope so." The old man's eyes sparkled with a bit of life. "With a church in the heart of Ascension Parish here on the bayou, I'd better know a thing or two."

Becka's eyes widened. "Did you say Ascension Parish?"

"Why, yes." The old man nodded. "You know Louisiana is divided into parishes. It's like counties in other states. And this parish is called Ascension."

Becka and Scott exchanged glances. They had had numerous encounters with the occult through a New Age bookstore back home called the Ascension Bookshop.

"Now tell me, what do you want to know about voodoo, child?" Pastor Barchett asked.

Becka told him everything: how Z had sent them to help Sara Thomas, about their experiences with the occult in California. She even described the necklace Sara wore.

The old pastor leaned back in his chair, closed his eyes, and thought for a long moment.

Then the moment became longer.

And longer still . . .

Finally, Scott whispered to his sister, "I think he fell asleep."

At the sound of Scott's voice, the old man's eyes popped opened. "I think I have your answer."

"You do?!" they both exclaimed at the same time. They leaned forward so as not to miss a single word of the wisdom he was about to speak.

Pastor Barchett hesitated just a moment and then answered, "Pray."

Scott and Becka blinked. They remained silent, waiting for the rest of the answer. But there was nothing else.

"Pray?" Scott said. "That's it? Just pray?"

The pastor nodded. "And believe. Pray that God will show Sara the error of her ways, that she will repent. And believe that he has sent you for a purpose that will not be thwarted."

Scott and Becka glanced at one another in exasperation. Another dead end.

ℕ

Once outside, it was Becka's turn to show disgust. "Pray?" she said. "Pray?? We could've done that at Aunt Myrna's. We could have done that in *California.*"

"*And* believe," Scott snorted, shaking his head. "Don't forget believe. It's just the same pat answer we've heard a million times before."

Becka nodded. She knew it was good advice. There was nothing wrong with praying and believing. Still, she had to agree that the pastor's advice was pretty much a formula answer and not very helpful in their particular situation.

"Hey! There she is!"

Becka looked up to see Scott pointing toward Sara Thomas. She had left the library and was heading down the street.

"Come on!" Becka said.

"What?"

Becka started forward. Before she would admit defeat, she had to try one last time. "Sara, Sara! . . . Wait up!"

The girl looked over in surprise—and annoyance. "What do you want?" she demanded as Becka arrived at her side.

"I, uh . . . I thought maybe, you know, if you were going to lunch, maybe we could sort of treat you."

"You don't think I can afford lunch?"

Becka faltered. "No, that's not it. I just . . . well, it's sort of . . . you know . . . to make up for getting off . . . ," the words were coming harder now, "on the wrong . . . foot. . . ."

For a brief second, something softened in Sara's eyes. Like she appreciated the thought. Like she really wanted to talk. But suddenly, she reached for her stomach and doubled over.

"Hey!" Scott said, moving to her side. "Are you all right?"

"Get away from me—both of you!"

Becka was taken aback. "Sara, are you sure you're—?"

"Leave me alone!" She shoved Becka away hard—so hard that Becka stumbled back and fell against a lamppost. That hurt a bit, but not enough to stop her from heading toward the girl again until—

"I'm warning you." Sara was still doubled over and gasping for breath. "If you don't stay away from me, the next time . . . the next time you'll really get hurt." Then, struggling to stand up straight, she turned and ran down the street.

"Sara!" Becka called after her. "Sara, come back!"

But she didn't stop.

Slowly Becka turned to Scott. She wondered if he was thinking the exact thing she was: *What did Sara mean by "The next time you'll really get hurt"?*

Becka knew. It was one of two things: either the bruise she'd received from the lamppost or . . .

. . . or Sara Thomas was aware of everything that had been happening to them—the near accidents . . . the near-fatal accidents. If these accidents were really someone's attempts to scare off Becka and Scott, then they'd failed so far. But would they succeed "the next time"?

The next time you'll really get hurt.

Becka could feel a chill creep over her body. All morning she had been fighting the fear, trying to keep it at bay. But now it flooded in. She didn't feel strong enough to stop it. The plane, the thresher, and the bus—these were more than coincidences. Scott was right—something was happening. Something was pursuing them—something more powerful and evil than they had ever encountered before.

And if they didn't back off, if they didn't stop now, it could destroy them.

"Beck . . . Beck, you all right?"

She met her brother's concerned gaze and tried to smile but couldn't. "Let's get out of here," she whispered. Sara's words echoed in her head: *The next time you'll really get hurt.* "Let's get out of here now."

4

he trip back to
Aunt Myrna's was sad. It was one of the few
times Scott and Becka had ever admitted
defeat. They knew they'd lost. Not only did
Sara not want their help, whatever power she
was caught up in was far too powerful for
them to battle. Z had overestimated their
strength. They could not fight this enemy.

And if they tried, they knew they would be seriously injured.

Becka wondered why it was different this time; why they felt so powerless, so overwhelmed. Maybe they were missing something. But when she tried to think it through, Sara's ominous words mocked her.

The next time you'll really get hurt.

When they arrived back at the farm, John Garrett waited to take them on the tour he had promised. But things had changed considerably in the last twenty-four hours. Neither Scott nor Becka was particularly thrilled about the idea.

Scott was able to beg off, making some excuse about his ankle. And, as much as Becka wanted to find her own reason not to go, part of her knew the walk would do her good.

Besides, she would no longer be in danger. It was over. They were no longer pursuing Sara. Evil had won. And now as long as they didn't bother it, it wouldn't bother them. The war was over. Peace had been declared—a peace that left Sara as its victim.

That thought bothered Becka, but there was nothing she could do now. She pushed it out of her mind as she followed John past the sugarcane and into the woods.

The place was breathtaking. River waters

had molded the low, flat swamplands for thousands of years. Vegetation grew wildly, enclosing everything in dim, leafy vaulted chambers. As she followed John Garrett deeper into the foliage, she almost felt as though she had entered an inner sanctum where the sun was an intruder. Plants grew everywhere. Mosses, vines, trees, algae, ferns. Everything had life.

And the flowers smelled richer in here than anywhere else she'd ever been before.

Becka felt as though she were in a holy place, a great cathedral of nature, where speaking was forbidden. She stopped for a moment and took a deep breath. "It's . . . beautiful," she whispered. "Beyond beautiful."

John sat on a nearby log. "Always is. Some people get used to it, I suppose, but not me. Every time I come here, I feel like I did the first time I saw it."

Becka nodded. In the distance she heard a rumbling. "Is that thunder?"

"Could be. Kinda feels like it." He looked at the trees. The leaves waved in the sudden breeze. "Suppose we better get you back before the storm hits. It doesn't last long, but in these parts, when it rains, it rains."

"Oh, not yet!" Becka protested. "It's so beautiful. Can't we stay just a few more minutes?"

John shrugged. "If you don't mind gettin' wet."

There was another rumble. Closer this time.

"I don't mind."

"Me neither." John grinned. "Nothing like a good shower to wash away your cares and make you feel alive."

Becka nodded. She needed that more than he knew. She looked up and breathed in deeply. Everything about this place made her feel free, alive. She couldn't help grinning.

"What?" John asked.

"Nothing."

"No, tell me."

"It's just . . . all this beauty makes me . . . I don't know . . . more aware of . . . God— of how powerful he is and how much he loves us."

John broke into an easy smile. "Me, too. Guess that's why I never got too caught up in all that voodoo stuff we were talking about yesterday."

The word *voodoo* brought reality crashing back into Becka's mind. Poor Sara. She would never experience this freedom. She would never taste and enjoy this love. The image of Sara, frightened and alone, fingering the doll around her neck, would not leave Becka's thoughts.

"John?"

"Yes?"

"What does it mean when someone wears a small cloth doll around their neck?"

There was another rumble. Much closer. She looked up. The branches overhead swayed in the wind.

"Might mean nothing." John stood up and started down the path. Becka followed. "But round here, that's what an initiate does."

"An initiate?"

"Someone newly admitted into the cult." Becka's heart sank.

A gentle tapping began as drops of water struck the leaves overhead and dripped through the canopy in little streams. But it didn't matter. Becka had volunteered to be soaked, and soaked she would be.

The deeper they went into the woods, the thicker the vegetation became, until at one point, the swamp on each side of them was covered from bank to bank with plants. It reminded Becka of a beautiful, jade green blanket.

"Oh, look!" She pointed to a patch of vivid pink flowers. Even in the downpour they seemed to shimmer. "What are those called?"

"Got me." John shrugged. "You can find lots of 'em around back in here."

"They're so beautiful." She took a step or

two toward them until John swung out and grabbed her arm. "Be careful."

She looked to him quizzically until he pointed to the green carpet she was about to step on. He stuck his toe into it to show that it was actually water. "Don't want to go in there. You'll find lots of critters you don't want to tangle with."

Becka nodded her thanks and looked back over to the flowers. Too bad. They were so beautiful.

John turned and continued leading her down the path.

Once again thoughts of Sara flooded Becka's mind until a sudden clap of thunder caused her to jump.

The rain came down even harder. Becka tilted her head back and let it pour over her face. It was refreshing.

But still, there was Sara.

"John!" she shouted over the pounding rain. "Do you know a girl named Sara Thomas?"

John shook his head. "Don't think so."

"I think she might be part of Big Sweet's—"

"Shhh!" John cut her off. Before Becka could react, he resumed speaking. "I don't know anybody named Sara! You shouldn't be talking about Big Sweet in here!" His voice was barely discernible over the pouring water.

Lightning flashed, followed by an immediate explosion of thunder that caused Becka's ears to ring.

"You see that over there?" John pointed toward the woods.

Becka peered through the rain, but the downpour was too heavy to make out anything.

But John kept his hand outstretched. She stared at the spot until she finally saw two bald cypress trees rising into the air.

"I see a couple of trees!" she shouted.

"Between them!" he yelled. "Look between them!"

Ever so faintly through the sheets of falling water, Becka caught a glimpse of something. "Is it a cabin?" she shouted.

John Garrett nodded. "That's Big Sweet's place. I never go farther than this."

Becka looked at him. There was no missing the concern in his eyes. She turned back to peer at the trees through the rain. There was another flash of lightning. For the briefest second she saw the cabin.

Suddenly she felt very cold, very wet—and very frightened.

~

Over at Sorrento the rain was just beginning to come down. But the baseball coach wasn't about to let a little water stop his boys from practicing.

It must have seemed strange to see Sara Thomas sitting by herself up in the bleachers, no umbrella, the only one sitting in the rain to watch. But Sara had important business to attend to.

Behind the backstop, John Noey swung hard at a pitch and connected. The ball sailed high over the pitcher's head and deep into center field.

"Nice hit, Noey!" Coach yelled. "Nice hit!"

On the mound the pitcher took another windup and delivered another fastball. This time John sent it into left field, even farther than the last one. At sixteen, John was bigger than most of the guys his age and easily the best hitter on Sorrento High's team.

In the stands, Sara, who was growing wetter by the second, reached into her purse and pulled out a doll. This one was also made of cloth but was much larger than the one she wore around her neck.

And it was wearing a baseball uniform.

John Noey stepped out of the batter's box, wiped his bat on a towel, then scuffed his shoes on the ground the way he'd seen the pros do. Noey was cocky, to be sure, but it was more than that. Being a star athlete in high school had given him a brash machismo usually found in much older boys.

Stepping back into the box, he nodded to the pitcher.

Sara held the doll in her left hand while she dug in her purse with the other. For a second she panicked, thinking she'd lost it. But then she felt it and pulled out a large hatpin.

Noey stood confidently as the pitcher wound up to deliver another fastball.

In the stands Sara began quietly chanting something over and over. She placed the doll beside her on the bleacher. The chant grew louder. She raised the hatpin high. Then, at the peak of her chant, she jammed the pin hard into the doll's head.

The ball had left the pitcher's hand. It was coming in hard and high.

Water suddenly dribbled from John's cap. He blinked once, taking his eye off the speeding ball. But that was all it took. He didn't see it suddenly veer up and inside. He tried to duck, but he was too late. The ball crashed into his forehead at seventy-four miles an hour.

John Noey collapsed into the mud.

Players raced to him. The coaches shoved players aside to get to him. But Noey was going nowhere. He was unconscious. Maybe for good.

Sara Thomas smiled. "Home run," she whispered, feeling a rush of power sweep over her. Revenge was sweet. But she wasn't finished.

Not by a long shot.

Becka knew that she would get yelled at for staying out in the rain. Her soaked clothes and the chilly wind from the storm could make anyone sick. In fact, when she sloshed through the family room and up the stairs, even Scott rolled his eyes at her foolishness.

After a hot shower and a change into dry clothes, she joined her brother down at the computer. "Any word from Z?" she asked.

Scott shook his head. "Not a thing." He reached over, shut off the computer, and let out a long, slow sigh. "We blew it, Beck. It's over."

Becka nodded sadly.

"Whatever's been happening to us is way out of our league. We've run into stuff more powerful than we can handle. I mean, it's one thing to deal with supposed ghosts and Ouija boards. But how do we deal with something that can drop a plane out of the sky or make a bus spin like a top? And now even Z's flaking out on us."

"Problems?"

At the quietly spoken question, the two glanced up and found Mom standing in the doorway of the family room. She'd just finished helping Aunt Myrna with the dishes and had come to join her children.

When neither of them answered her question, she sat on the sofa and tried again. "Scotty says this is the toughest case you've had."

"You've got that right," Becka said. "For starters, the girl we're supposed to be helping—Sara Thomas—doesn't even want our help."

Mom nodded. "That's hard. But not unusual."

"What do you mean?"

"Lots of times the people who need help are the ones who don't want it. Like Julie. Or Krissi."

Becka stared at her mother. She was right! How had she forgotten the resistance they'd met anytime they'd tried to help someone caught up in the occult?

Mom went on. "What did Z say?"

"That's another thing," Scott said. "He won't talk to us. He sends us out here all on our own and then just abandons us."

"He didn't give you any advice?"

"Just that we're suppose to pray, believe, and not give in to our fears."

"And he mentioned the pastor," Becka reminded him.

"Oh yeah." Scott's tone was filled with scorn. "The pastor. Z said the local pastor would help."

"And?"

"All he came up with was 'Pray and believe.'" Scott shook his head. "Can you believe that? Just 'pray and believe.'"

Mom frowned slightly. "Sounds like pretty solid advice."

"Well, yeah . . . I mean . . . I know," Scott said, blinking. "But we've only heard it a million times."

"So you've done it already, then?"

Scott blinked again. "Done it?"

Mom tilted her head. "Prayed."

Scott and Becka looked at each other, then at their mother.

"Uh, well, no . . . ," Scott admitted hesitantly.

"Not exactly," Becka added. "We've been . . . busy." But even as she said it, she knew it was a lame excuse.

Mom nodded. "Well, I've got time now, if you're interested."

"For what?"

"Well, to pray, of course."

"Here?" Becka asked. "Now?"

"Can you think of a better time?"

The brother and sister glanced at each other a little sheepishly. Becka laughed softly. She couldn't believe it. In all their hurry and determination to be the great teen ghost busters, they had forgotten a couple of very important ingredients: to pray and believe. Pastor Barchett had reminded them about those ingredients. She grinned. Maybe he wasn't as out of it as they'd thought.

"Sure," Becka said while Scott nodded. They moved to the couch, bowed their heads, and began to pray with Mom.

~

In the dream, Sara wore a wedding veil. She looked beautiful all in white. Her face glowed with anticipation as she walked down the aisle toward her future husband. Though the groom's back was to her, she knew he would be perfect.

Everything in this dream was perfect.

There was her mother in the first pew. She was as healthy and vibrant as she had been before she got sick. And there by her side was her father—handsome and proud like he had been before he started drinking.

Everything was just the way she'd always hoped it would be. . . .

Until the groom turned around.

A thick red horn protruded from his forehead, and his face was black and blistered as if it had been charred. But it was the eyes that terrified her most. Huge and black. Staring at them was like looking into deep wells. Wells that had no bottom. Only horror. Deep, dark, everlasting horror.

Sara woke up screaming.

She fell back against the pillow, her chest heaving with ragged breaths, and closed her eyes in an effort to go back to sleep. She couldn't. The dreams had been coming more and more frequently. And with them came the nausea—the same nausea she had felt when talking with the two kids from California.

There was only one way to take her mind off the nausea. And the monster. To think back to the beautiful woman she had seen in the dream. To remember how things had been when her mother was alive, before she got sick and died, before her father buried his grief in alcohol . . . before her life had been ripped out from under her.

Hot tears sprang to her eyes. Thinking about the past was always like this. But that was OK. Sooner or later the crying would tire her out and she would fall asleep. That's how it worked most nights. She hoped it would tonight.

5

$\mathcal{S}$ara Thomas
knew that Ronnie Fitzgerald would show up
at Janet Baylor's sweet-sixteen party. Janet
was the most popular girl in school. Sara was
surprised to have even been invited. Apparently Janet had decided to invite the entire
sophomore class, even the poor Raggedy
Ann whom everyone ignored.

Sara spent most of the evening off by herself, secretly spying on Ronnie and watching for the right moment.

Earlier she had hollowed out a large candle and buried a lock of Ronnie's hair in the wax along with a slip of paper on which she had written "Worst Luck" and "Ronnie Fitzgerald" seven times. She then dug a small hole in a field near Ronnie's house in a place where the moonlight would shine on it. She buried the bottom half of the candle in the hole, lit the wick, and went home.

All of this was according to the instructions the *hungan* had given her. The hardest part had been getting the lock of hair, but even that proved easier than she had expected. All she had done was sit behind him on the bus, and when he leaned his head back, she snipped off a piece.

He never even knew.

Many of the kids at the party had started changing into their swimsuits and jumping into the Baylors' large pool. Ronnie wasn't out there yet, but Sara knew he soon would be. He wouldn't miss a chance to show off his body and his diving skills.

Sara moved closer to the patio doors so she could get a better view of the crowd around the pool. It was then that she heard someone crying. Cautiously she peered around the kitchen door and listened to an older woman talking with Mrs. Baylor.

"They say they don't know. . . . He might never wake up!" the older woman sobbed.

"Try not to worry, Amelia. John's in good hands," Mrs. Baylor said. "He's in the best hospital in the county."

Sara felt a pang of guilt jab into her gut. That had to be John Noey's mother. So, he was still in a coma that he might never come out of?

"I know he's not always a good boy," Mrs. Noey said, wiping her nose. "But he lost his papa when he was little, you know. He never got over it. He loved his papa so much. . . . He's been angry at the world ever since. But he's always helped take care of me and his little sister. He's like a daddy to little Gina. She was just a baby when Ralph died. John's tried hard to make it up to her."

Sara's head spun, and her heart filled with remorse. She'd never given a thought to John Noey's family and how they might feel. She never considered how losing him might affect their lives.

Sara drifted away from the kitchen, trying hard not to hear Mrs. Noey's sobs. Out of the corner of her eye she saw Ronnie Fitzgerald bouncing high on the diving board. Her eyes widened in horror.

Oh, no! I don't want this now! Not after what happened to John. No! Don't let—!

But it happened. Ronnie—the perfect athlete, the expert diver—lost his footing on a high jump and flipped backward instead of forward. Thrown back onto the board, he struck his head with a hard thump.

The blow was so solid that Sara heard it through the patio glass. Nearly sick with guilt and horror, she watched the unconscious Ronnie roll off the board and strike his head again on the side of the pool before tumbling into the water.

People rushed to his aid. Sara heard someone say something about not moving him. A couple of girls screamed over the blood.

She couldn't look. All she could do was turn and walk away, wondering if she would ever stop feeling totally awful.

~

The following morning Becka was sick. The wind and rain from Saturday afternoon had taken their toll.

"You look terrible," Scott said as she arrived at the breakfast table.

She sniffed and mumbled something about his looking in a mirror once in a while himself.

"Are you feeling all right, dear?" Aunt

Myrna asked as she shoved a plate of eggs, a thick slice of ham, and grits under Becka's nose.

"It's just a little cold," Becka mumbled through a sniffle. It wasn't exactly a lie, but it wasn't the truth either. Whatever she was coming down with was going to be bad. One good clue was the way her stomach was turning at the smell of the food. Or the way her head was already starting to ache.

"So, what are we going to do with our next three days off?" Scott asked as he started on his second bowl of grits.

"I think ..." Becka sniffed again—"I think we should give Sara one last chance."

"Beck . . ." Scott started to protest.

"I know, I know. We said it was over, but don't you think we should at least give her one more try? And this time, maybe do it the right way?"

Scott gave her a look. "You mean like the pastor said—with prayer and believing?"

Becka nodded. "That's what Z said, too—remember?"

Scott gave a loud sigh. It was a sound she recognized—one that said he was really put out with her. But as she glanced at him, she saw the gleam in his eyes. He knew that she was right. No doubt about it.

There were many dancers at the ceremony, but Sara danced the wildest of all. Her movements were frenzied, driven, as though she were stomping all her troubles into the earth.

Suddenly she couldn't breathe. She choked, gasping for air. The other dancers came to a stop and stared as she gagged, pointing at her throat in a silent plea for help.

No one moved.

She dropped to her knees, motioning frantically. Everything grew fuzzy and white, then whiter and whiter until she crumpled to the ground.

A large African-American man rose from an old wicker chair that looked like some sort of throne. Sara watched hazily as he came to kneel over her, placing his fingers on her neck as though feeling for a pulse.

At last he looked up and spoke. "Sara is dead. She defied the gods. She has been struck down."

Sara wanted to argue, to disagree, but she could not seem to open her mouth or move her body.

Suddenly she felt herself being lifted up. But now she was no longer herself. Somehow she had become somebody else.

Now she was John Noey!

She lay in a hospital bed hearing her mother weep over her. No, not *her* mother. *John Noey's* mother. She tried to move but could not. She could still hear. She could still feel. She knew all that was going on around her, but she could not move.

John Noey could not move.

Hot tears fell onto her arms as the mother began to sob and cry over her.

"I'm sorry," a doctor's voice said. "We've done all we can do."

She felt a sheet pulled over her face. Dead! John Noey had just been declared dead!

But she was alive! She had to tell them! John Noey was still alive. Only now she wasn't John Noey.

Now she was Ronnie Fitzgerald!

Wires covered her body. Tubes stuck into her nose and mouth—no, *his* nose and mouth. She was alone. All alone. Just the quiet blip of the heart monitor over her head. And the rhythmic sound of the air as it was being pushed in and out of her lungs by a respirator.

Suddenly the heart monitor started blipping irregularly. She panicked, tried to move, but there was nothing she could do. She could feel the heart inside her chest pounding like a jackhammer gone berserk. Then it stopped altogether. So did the blips

on the monitor. Now there was nothing but
a long, loud whine.

She tried to breathe but couldn't. She
tried to scream, but no words would come.
Soon she heard people racing around her
and someone shouting, "He's flat-lining!
We're going to lose him!"

Sara was desperate to move, to breathe.
She silently choked until—

She sat bolt upright, awake and coughing.

When she caught her breath, she glanced
around the classroom. More than a few stu-
dents stared at her. Several smirked. She
had fallen asleep in class again. This was not
surprising, since she'd given up sleeping
during the night in an effort to stop the
dreams. But apparently that didn't matter
now.

The dreams were coming during the day,
whenever she closed her eyes and started to
doze. Day or night, the dreams came.

Sara looked at the clock. It was almost
three o'clock. She was anxious to leave. All
this time she'd thought revenge on the boys
would make her feel better. It didn't. It made
her feel worse. The sobs of John's mother
and the sound of Ronnie slamming into the
board echoed in her mind.

But Sara felt more than guilt. She also felt
afraid. Now she knew the power of voodoo.

She knew that it could turn back on her if she wasn't careful.

At last the bell sounded. Sara let out a sigh of relief. All day long the school had been getting reports on John's and Ronnie's conditions from the hospital. It was all anyone talked about. Both were in comas in ICU. Sara wanted to get away—to go home and cover her head.

To sleep.

These were the only thoughts running through her mind as she headed toward the bus.

"Sara! Excuse me! Sara Thomas?"

Someone called her. She turned and saw the same girl and her brother who had bothered her a couple of days before, waiting at the bottom of the steps. *Oh, no!* Sara thought. *They're the last people I want to see!*

Becka stepped forward. "Sara, it's us again, Rebecca and Scott. Listen, I just want to say something. It may not be any of my business, but if you're messing around with—"

"Then leave, OK?" Sara cut her off. "If it's none of your business, then you and your creepy brother can just—"

"I just wanted to warn you," Becka interrupted. "If you're messing around with voodoo, you could be losing control of your life."

Sara's eyes grew wild. "Why are you trying

to hurt me?" she demanded. Her voice sounded shrill. She knew others were listening but didn't care. "You want to take away my powers, don't you?"

Becka reached toward her. "Sara—"

"No! I'm warning you for the last time. Leave me alone!"

Now it was Scott's turn. "Listen, we're not trying to hurt you or take away any—"

"You bet you won't! 'Cause I won't let you." Sara reached inside her purse and pulled out the scissors she had used to cut Ronnie's hair. "Get out of my way!"

Becka froze. "All right, Sara, we'll leave. But couldn't we just—?"

Suddenly Sara lunged at her. "I warned you!"

Becka jerked backward, lost her footing, and fell hard onto the sidewalk. Sara swooped down at her with the scissors.

"Stop!" Scott tried to block her, but she was too fast.

But instead of stabbing Becka, Sara suddenly cut off a lock of her hair.

Rising to her feet, she shouted, "I curse you! Worst luck will befall you! *Pire* sort! *Pire* chance! *Pire* fortune!" She started backing away. "Worst luck! Worst luck! Worst luck! will be worse for you than it was for John Ronnie."

Sara spun around and started running. Her heart pounded in her chest. She had to get away. The magic was about to begin. She did not want to stay around and watch Rebecca suffer.

~

Scott helped his sister to her feet. "You OK?"

Becka nodded. "Yes, just sort of stunned . . . that was weird! She cut my hair!"

"I know," Scott said. "Nothing like being cursed to really trash a day. C'mon. I think we'd better get home."

"But the bus to Aunt Myrna's isn't due for another hour."

"I mean *home* home," Scott replied. "Back to California."

By the time they got to the bus stop, Becka felt a lot worse. Maybe it was the emotion, or maybe it was the fever she knew had been rising steadily all morning. Whatever the case, when she reached the bus stop, Becka had to sit on a bench.

"Can I get you anything?" Scott asked. "A Coke or something?"

She could see that he was worried. "Maybe some juice," she said.

"All right. I'll check the gas station over there. Just wait here." Scott quickly headed across the street.

Becka dreaded the bus ride back to Aunt Myrna's. The jouncing of that old bus would only make her feel worse. She closed her eyes. The throbbing in her head was unbearable.

She opened her eyes and glanced at an abandoned newspaper lying beside her on the bench. It was *The Sorrento Times*. The headline read *"Second Sorrento High Student in Coma."*

Despite her throbbing headache, Becka forced herself to read on. Ronnie Fitzgerald had been injured on Sunday night; John Noey, the day before that. Both boys were in the hospital, barely clinging to life. Both had been the victims of strange accidents that, according to the paper, "many in the area believe were due to religious rituals."

Suddenly Sara's words came screaming back into her mind: *It will be worse for you than it was for John and Ronnie.*

Her eyes shifted back to the paper, scanning for the injured boys' names again. There they were. Ronnie Fitzgerald and John Noey.

Becka's vision blurred. The trees and people around her started to move. She felt worse than she thought. The fever, the headache, the encounter with Sara all contributed to that. And now this.

It will be worse for you.

Fear continued to grow, consuming her, fogging her thinking.

Next time you'll really be hurt.

Fear after fear had piled up since even before they had landed. She tried to focus her eyes, but it was impossible. The people, the trees, the buildings seemed to spin around her.

It will be worse.

She could feel herself growing clammy with icy perspiration.

Worst luck! Worst luck!

She was going to faint. She knew it.

I curse you! I curse you!

She was going to—

Suddenly she felt her body tilt forward. She tried to stop herself but couldn't. A moment later, she toppled onto the sidewalk.

Rebecca Williams had passed out.

6

When Becka woke up, she found herself lying on the bench with Scott and Pastor Barchett standing over her. "But you'll pray for her, won't you, Pastor?" Scott was asking.

Pastor Barchett nodded. "Of course I will. But you have the authority of prayer also. Curses and spells have no power over Christians unless we give it to them."

Becka moved and tried to sit up.

"Beck, you're awake. Are you all right?" Scott asked. "I ran over and got the pastor."

"How are you feeling, my dear?" Pastor Barchett asked.

"I feel better, I think," she said, though she was still a little woozy.

"Maybe you should see a doctor," Pastor Barchett offered.

"I'm all right," Becka said. "It's just . . . well, I haven't felt real good all day. With Sara attacking me, and all that's been happening to us, and then reading in the newspaper about those two Sorrento High boys and their freak accidents . . ."

Pastor Barchett nodded. "Both are classmates of Sara's, I've heard. I'm afraid it sounds like more than a coincidence to me, too."

"I think I'll be all right now," Rebecca repeated. "Did we miss our bus?"

Scott shook his head. "Should be here any sec. Unless . . ." He turned to the pastor. "I don't suppose you'd drive us home?"

Pastor Barchett laughed. "No, they've long since stopped letting me drive a car. My eyes are bad. But I'm sure I can find someone to take you."

"I'll be fine on the bus," Becka assured

them. "It's just a short ride. But what should we do about Sara?"

"Keep praying," Pastor Barchett said, "and believing. But remember, you can't deliver someone from something if they don't want to be free. They have to want it."

"Well, she's made it pretty clear that she doesn't," Scott said. "Sounds like Z really missed the boat this time. How could God possibly want us to visit Sara when she doesn't even want to listen?"

"What about Moses and Pharaoh?" Pastor Barchett asked. "God sent Moses, didn't he? And what about the prophets? Just because the people didn't listen doesn't mean God didn't send them."

Becka leaned forward. She was still feeling a little light-headed, but she wasn't about to admit it. "I think we should give it a couple more days," she said.

"Becka . . . ," Scott protested.

"Two more days," she repeated.

Pastor Barchett nodded in agreement. "And in the meantime, keep praying . . . and believing."

~

By the time they returned to the farm, Scott had to argue with Becka to get her to take a nap.

"But I feel good now," Becka insisted. "In fact, I'd like to go for a walk. I want to show you these pretty flowers I saw in the swamp."

"A walk?!" Scott exclaimed. "No way! You have to lie down and rest!"

"Stop acting like Mom!" she snapped. "I feel fine!"

"All right," Scott said. "If you won't listen to me, let's talk to Mom and see what she says."

Becka panicked. "No! Don't tell Mom! She'll make me stay in bed for a week!"

"Then take a nap."

"If I take a nap, will you walk with me into the woods so we can smell those pink flowers?"

Scott made a face. "Flowers?! What do I care about flowers?"

"There's lots of other stuff, too. It's really cool. Please?"

Scott hesitated.

"I'll owe you," she promised.

"All right," Scott finally agreed. "But you have to rest first."

"Will do."

But Becka couldn't sleep. She still felt a little foggy. She knew the fever hadn't left. She also knew something else: although she pretended it wasn't true, her fear of Sara and her powers was still very, very strong. Probably *too* strong.

Then there were the other thoughts—the ones that had been growing more powerful every hour. These thoughts urged her to go into the swamp and smell those incredible pink flowers.

～

On Sara Thomas's bedroom dresser was a glass full of those incredible pink flowers. Buried in the midst of them was the lock of Becka's hair. And underneath the flowers?

Underneath the flowers was a live snake.

～

An hour later, Becka and Scott set off for the woods and swamp. Becka couldn't explain it. Even though she still felt weak, finding those flowers and seeing their beautiful color had become very important. It was like a craving, something she couldn't stop wanting.

She led the way. For a while they followed the path she had taken with John Garrett. But each time she thought she saw a glimpse of the pink flowers, she veered a little farther off until, before she knew it, they were on a path she'd never seen before—a path surrounded by thick vegetation.

They continued forward for several minutes until they spotted a large clearing in the distance.

It looked like some sort of gathering place. A dozen logs were arranged in a huge circle. The pink flowers grew all around the clearing.

"Wow! Cool place!" Scott exclaimed. "You never told me about this."

"I've never seen it before," Becka said. "I must've taken a wrong turn back there."

"What do you think this was?" Scott asked as he explored the area. "Maybe a Native American church or something? It looks ancient."

Becka barely heard him. Instead, she walked along the logs, stopping every so often to smell one of the flowers. "Aren't they beautiful?"

"What?"

"The flowers. Aren't they beautiful?"

"Yeah. Beautiful. You know, Beck, those flowers are all you've talked about since we came out here."

"They're so beautiful."

"What's the matter with you?" Before she could answer, Scott's eyes landed on something else—a large, makeshift altar made of flat gray stones. "Hey, check it out!"

They ran to it but suddenly came to a stop.

"Is that red stain what I think it is?" Scott asked.

Becka nodded, glancing around. "Don't see any flowers here."

"Beck, I'm pretty sure that's blood. And look here. There's some kind of animal hair sticking to the rock. Something was killed here recently. . . . Somebody's using this place for animal sacrifices." Scott stepped back as the memory of his terrifying dream about the goat came rushing back.

"Let's go look for more flowers," Becka said.

Her words pulled Scott from his momentary shock. He looked at his sister long and hard. Something was up. He was feeling more uneasy by the second. "I think we'd better get you home."

This time Scott took the lead. He headed out of the clearing and searched for the path. But after about thirty feet, he stopped cold and pointed at something in a nearby ditch. "Look, Beck!"

Becka joined him. "More flowers?"

Scott didn't respond. He just stood and stared. In the pit were the remains of a slaughtered goat.

"Oh . . . that's terrible!" Becka said.

"Guess we know now why Aunt Myrna's goat hasn't come home," Scott said sadly. "Big Sweet slaughtered him in one of his rituals."

"We should go."

"You're right." Scott headed toward what he hoped was Aunt Myrna's farm.

Becka stopped suddenly. "No. We should go and look for more flowers."

Scott spun around to look at Becka. Her face was flushed and her eyes looked glazed. The unease in the pit of his stomach became full-blown concern, then anger. Something had happened to Becka. And whatever was wrong with his sister was getting worse by the minute. He had to get her out of there. But as he looked around, he had a sinking feeling that they were lost. He was sure of it.

"Becka? Beck, I think we'd better pray. I think—"

But when he turned back to her, she was gone.

"Becka!" he shouted, looking around. He began to panic, running first one way, then the other. "Becka!" he shouted again. *Dear God,* he prayed, *don't let me lose her. Not in here!* "Becka!"

But she was nowhere to be found. Desperately he continued the search. Plants were everywhere. Spanish moss hung down thick in his face. Everything looked the same. He had no idea where he was or if he'd been running around in circles.

"Becka! Beck—"

Then he heard the sound of splashing. And he knew as certainly as if he'd seen it happen—Becka had jumped into the water.

"*Becka!*"

He raced along a log, following the sound.

"Becka! Becka!"

At last he saw her. She was up to her neck in the water a few feet from the shore.

"What are you doing?!" he demanded.

She didn't answer. Instead, she treaded water, moving *away* from him.

"Becka!!"

A moment later he had his answer. She reached out and grabbed a handful of the pink flowers.

"See?" she called. "Flowers!"

"Yes, very nice." It was all Scott could do to contain himself. "Now if you don't mind, would you hurry up and get out of there? We've got to—"

Suddenly he saw movement in the water. It looked like a log drifting across the swamp. But it was no log. His heart began pounding. It was an alligator! And it was swimming right for his sister!

"More flowers over here!" she called, starting to paddle even farther away.

"No, Beck! Come back! Get out of there! Look over your shoulder!"

Becka did, but she seemed oblivious to the

approaching gator. Its two large, yellow eyes headed straight toward her.

"Look, Scotty." She pointed past the gator toward another group of flowers. "More flowers."

Scott was beside himself. "Nooo!" he screamed from the shore. "Look, Beck! I've got flowers here!" He scrambled around the shore scooping up flowers wherever he saw them. "See, Beck? I've got bigger ones—prettier ones! See? Right over here!"

Becka turned and saw Scott waving his handful of flowers. She smiled vacantly and began swimming back to him.

It was too late.

Her pace was no match for the gator, which rapidly closed the distance between them. It would be on her in seconds.

"Oh, God!" Scott cried. "Please save Beck! In the name of Jesus, please save her! Please . . ."

The alligator was only a few feet from her now. Its mouth opened wide, preparing to attack, when suddenly—

BAM! BAM!

The shots cracked through the swamp like thunder.

At first Scott was unsure what had happened. Then he saw the alligator roll over onto its back. Blood soon appeared in the water. Finally, the creature sank slowly under the green carpet of water and plants.

A sudden rustle of leaves caused Scott to spin around. A huge African-American man carrying a rifle soon appeared. Perched on his head was a battered straw hat. He chewed on a piece of sugarcane.

"It's all right now, missy," he called. "You can take your time comin' back. But you best get outta there soon as possible. This area's got more gators than that old-timer."

Scott could only stare as Becka swam toward him. Once again she smiled vacantly.

When she arrived, the big man reached his hand out to help her. "Hello there, missy. Pleased to make your acquaintance. My name is Benjamin. But most folks in these parts call me Big Sweet."

7

*B*ig Sweet contin-
ued to hold out his hand to help Becka from
the swamp. She hesitated, remaining in the
chest-deep water.

"Flowers?" she asked.

The big man smiled. "What?"

"She's talking about these!" Scott called.
He was about thirty feet away, holding up a

handful of the pink flowers for Big Sweet to see. "She's obsessed with them. That's why she dove into the water."

Big Sweet nodded as if he understood. "Sounds like she's under some kind of spell."

Confused and growing more angry by the second, Scott crossed toward the man. "Yes, and you did it . . . or one of your people did!"

Big Sweet held up his hand. "Whoa, son. Easy. We can talk about all that later. But no matter what you've heard, I am still preferable to another alligator."

"What?"

"We must get this girl out of that water before we have more company."

Scott understood and quickly joined Big Sweet. He leaned over the bank and held out the flowers to his sister. "Here they are, Beck. Come and get 'em."

As Becka reached for the flowers, Scott and Big Sweet took her arms and pulled her out of the water. She was soaked and dripping with slime.

"Look at your leg," Scott said. "It's bleeding!"

"She must've cut it on a briar under the water," Big Sweet said. "You better come over to my cabin and let me clean that wound for you."

"I don't know," Scott said warily. "We

should be heading back. Just point the way
to Myrna Carmen's house and—"

"Look, son, if I wanted to harm you, you'd
already be dead. I could've let that gator eat
your friend here and shot you instead. Truth
is, I hate shooting gators. Ain't that many
more left. And we got plenty of kids. Especially Yankee kids out messing where they
don't belong."

Scott was unsure whether to be terrified or
angry. But suddenly Big Sweet broke into a
big, booming laugh. "Now, c'mon to my
place," he said, "and let me dress that wound
'fore your friend winds up with an infection."

Scott nodded. "OK. But don't try anything
funny."

Big Sweet laughed again, then turned and
made his way up a small hill. Scott followed
cautiously, taking Becka by the hand and
leading her carefully.

On the way to Big Sweet's cabin, Scott
introduced himself and Becka. He was surprised at how much Big Sweet already
seemed to know about them. He wondered
if Big Sweet had asked John Garrett about
them.

Big Sweet's cabin lay on the other side of
the hill. It looked foreboding on the outside,
but once inside, Scott was surprised to see
that it was small and cozy. He was also sur-

prised to discover that the man had a wife
and two cute little girls who were four and
six. In fact, the whole place looked suspi-
ciously normal.

Becka sat quietly, playing with her handful
of flowers while Big Sweet washed the blood
off her leg. "Why you keep looking around
like that?" Big Sweet asked. "You expect bats
to fly out of the closet?"

Scott almost smiled. "Something like that,
I guess. We've never been in a . . ." He
stopped in midsentence, unsure of what
words to use.

"In a *hungan's* house?" Big Sweet asked.
"Is that what you mean?"

Scott swallowed.

"Well, son, a *hungan* is just like anyone else
. . . most of the time. It's only during the
ceremony that the *loa* commune with the
hungan. Otherwise he's like anyone else."

"How can you say you commune with the
dead and call yourself normal?" Scott asked.
He knew he was being pretty direct, but after
all, this was the top man, the guy with all the
answers.

Big Sweet cocked his head and looked at
Scott. "What's a city kid like you know about
the *loa?*"

Scott shrugged. "Not much. I just like
studying stuff like that."

Big Sweet's thick eyebrows knitted into a frown. "Stuff like what?"

Usually words came easily to Scott, but now, with Big Sweet staring at him—looking through him actually—he wasn't sure how to answer. "I just . . . like to read about . . . weird stuff." Scott winced as soon as he had said the words. Calling someone's religion "weird stuff" was not too bright, especially if that someone happened to be the high priest and was two or three times your size.

Big Sweet's eyes narrowed. He looked meaner than ever . . . until he suddenly broke into the biggest laugh yet. "Weird stuff." He continued laughing. "Weird stuff. That's pretty good!"

Scott gave Big Sweet half a smile, then glanced at Becka. She did not say a word. She was too busy playing with the pink flowers.

Big Sweet reached for a bottle of alcohol and poured some onto a wad of cotton. "This might sting a bit," he warned. But as he swabbed the cut with alcohol, Becka didn't even react.

Big Sweet shook his head. "That's a powerful curse. May take some doing to break it."

"Ask Sara Thomas," Scott said. "She's the one who put the curse on her."

Big Sweet was taken aback. "Sara Thomas? How do you know—?" He stopped himself, then shook his head. "I must explain to you what is happening to Sara Thomas. You know about the *loa,* the dead spirits. Well, there are two kinds of *loa. Rada loas* and *petro loas.*"

Scott listened, feeling uneasy.

"*Rada loas* are good spirits that help a person do good. *Petro loas* are mean spirits that help them do evil."

"What's that got to do with Sara or my sis—?"

"Sara Thomas has been picked on all her life. She needed something to defend herself, to fight back. That's a *petro loa.* That's what she sought and—" he let out a sigh— "that's what she got—a spirit of revenge."

"So you put a curse on Sara, and Sara put one on my sister."

Big Sweet looked at Scott a moment, then shook his head. "I did not put a curse on Sara. She asked for help; I gave it to her. She got herself a powerful *petro loa,* though. A strong one. I'm afraid Sara's a *loa's cheval* now."

"A what?"

"That means horse, a horse for the spirit to ride. And there is not much she can do until it decides it wants to get off."

"What about my sister?"

Big Sweet thought a moment. "I've got a black root. It can break spells like—"

"I don't want any of that stuff!" Scott interrupted.

Big Sweet frowned, not understanding.

"She's a Christian," Scott explained.
"Curses have no power over Christians."

"So I see . . . ," Big Sweet said, motioning
to Becka, who still played with the flowers.

Scott faltered. "That is, unless we allow
someone or something else to have power
over us."

Big Sweet sat, waiting for more.

Scott continued. "A lot of weird stuff's
been happening to us. And Becka's been getting kinda spooked. And now with the fever
and all, and Sara's curse, I guess she just
started to give in and believe—"

"So what are you going to do?" Big Sweet
interrupted.

Scott swallowed. "I guess . . . pray."

"Pray?"

"Yes."

"Pray? That's it?"

"Well . . . yeah."

Big Sweet folded his arms. "OK, let me see."

"What? Here?" Scott asked.

"I would not be taking her back into the
swamp this way. But then again, if you don't
think it will work . . ."

Scott quickly rose to the occasion. "Oh, it
will work, all right. You bet it will work!"

Big Sweet grinned. "Then, I am waiting."

With growing determination, Scott pushed aside his apprehension and reached for Becka's hand. He bowed his head and closed his eyes. "Dear Lord . . ." He cleared his throat, still feeling a little self-conscious. "Dear Lord, please break the power of this curse. Please help Becka to see that she doesn't have to be under this or any spell because of what you did for us on the cross. Because you set us free and gave us an even greater power." Scott hesitated. Part of him wanted to make the prayer longer and more dramatic, maybe turn it into a mini-sermon. But he knew he said what needed to be said. That was enough. "I ask these things in the name of Jesus Christ. Amen."

Scott opened his eyes.

Big Sweet sat silent, waiting. "That was it?" he asked.

Scott nodded. "That's it."

"No root or balm or potion?"

Scott shook his head. "We don't use that stuff. We don't need it."

Big Sweet turned and stared hard at Becka, waiting.

Nothing happened.

"Missy?" Big Sweet called. "Missy, are you there?"

Ever so slowly, Becka turned her head.

Scott and Big Sweet held their breath.

At last Becka spoke. "Would you like a flower?"

Scott winced. Big Sweet smiled.

Becka continued, frowning slightly. "No? Then can I dump them somewhere? I think they're making me sick. I must be allergic to them or something." She looked around the room, blinking in confusion. "Hey, where are we?" She looked down at her soaked clothes. "And how did I get all wet?"

Scott let out a sigh of relief. Big Sweet laughed his big laugh.

"Hello, missy," the man said. "My name is Big Sweet."

Becka turned to Scott, a trace of panic in her voice. "Is he serious?"

Scott nodded. "It's OK. You were out of it for a while. Big Sweet saved your life. We came here so he could clean that gash on your leg, and . . . uh . . . well, I just prayed and broke Sara's curse."

Becka leaned back in her chair. She felt a little weak. And for good reason. It was all coming back to her now: the cravings, the wanderings, and Sara's curse. She rubbed her neck. It felt stiff and hot from the fever. "Boy, do I feel stupid."

Scott said, "Big Sweet says Sara is possessed by a violent spirit."

"A *petro loa,*" Big Sweet added. "There are good spirits and bad spirits that can possess a person and—"

"But possession is wrong," Becka interrupted.

Big Sweet looked at her.

She continued. "If there's one thing we've learned over the months, it's that any spirit that possesses someone is not a good spirit. Those spirits always cause a person to do evil. Only the Holy Spirit comes into a person's life and causes him to do good."

Big Sweet rubbed his chin. "For a couple of kids, you sure think you know a lot about spirits."

Becka and Scott exchanged glances. If he only knew . . .

Big Sweet went on. "I don't know what you got, but it is clear it has power. Breaking that curse with no roots or potions is mighty strong power."

"Our power doesn't come from some-*thing,*" Scott explained. "It comes from some-*one*—the Holy Spirit, like Beck said."

Big Sweet eyed him. "All right, then. If you really want to help Sara Thomas, you must come to the ceremony tonight. Her *petro loa* is a dangerous one. I tried talking to it, but it won't listen. I've tried to get its ancestors to talk to me, but—"

"You can't talk to the dead," Becka cut in.

Big Sweet was obviously growing impatient with all the interruptions. "You cannot? Then who have I been talking to every week all these years?"

Again Scott and Becka traded looks.

After a deep breath, Scott finally answered him. "Demons. You've been talking to demons who are using you for their own purposes."

Big Sweet stood up. "You kids give me a big headache! You better head back now. Miss Myrna will be worried."

"And Sara?" Scott asked.

"If you are serious 'bout helping Sara, then you come to our ceremony tonight."

~

Sara had spent most of the night tossing, turning, and groaning, thanks to a horrible nightmare. She woke up gasping for air, then jumped out of bed and hurried over to the dresser mirror to stare at her reflection. What she saw caused her to let out a scream.

In the mirror, snakes writhed in her hair. They vanished suddenly.

She sat on a nearby chair and stared at herself. She felt as if she had aged several years in the last few days.

Angrily she grabbed the small cloth doll

still hanging around her neck and broke the chain. She threw the doll on the floor, then hurriedly dressed.

But just before she left the room, she walked back over to where the doll lay on the floor and stared at it for a long moment. Then, although it was the last thing she wanted to do, she picked it up and put it in her purse.

She had to. She no longer had a choice.

~

Going to the ceremony was the last thing Becka and Scott wanted to do, especially given Becka's condition and all they'd been through. But they both agreed that it would be their last opportunity to help Sara. And like it or not, that was why they had been sent to Louisiana in the first place.

Before they left for the ceremony, both of them knew they needed a reminder of the power God had given them through Jesus. The events of the past days had shaken their trust and weakened their faith. There was only one way to build it back up. They grabbed their Bibles and headed for the porch.

"Hey, remember this?" Scott asked as he flipped to a well-worn page. He quickly read the verse: " 'The Spirit who lives in you is greater than the spirit who lives in the world.' "

"Yeah," Becka sighed. "Too bad I forgot that earlier." She looked at the page her finger rested on in her Bible. "Here's another one we'd better not forget: 'These signs will accompany those who believe: They will cast out demons in my name.'"

Scott nodded. " 'If you believe, you will receive whatever you ask for in prayer.'"

"Praying and believing," Becka mused. "Sounds exactly like what Z told us at the very beginning."

"And Mom *and* Aunt Myrna's pastor," Scott added.

Becka shook her head. "Funny how you can hear some stuff so much that pretty soon you don't even pay attention to it."

"Well, we're paying attention now," Scott said as he stood. "Nothing's going to make us back down tonight."

"Scotty?"

"No, sir, we're going to get in there and bust some heads . . ."

"Scotty?"

". . . and show them they're not messing around with just any—"

"Scotty!"

"What?"

"Before we go, shouldn't we, like . . . you know . . . pray first?"

"Oh . . ."

For the first time she could remember, Becka actually thought she saw her brother blush.

"Yeah, of course." He cleared his throat. "I, uh, I knew that."

She gave him a grin as he sat back down. And there, together, brother and sister bowed their heads to pray for God's protection. They asked God's forgiveness for their wavering faith and pride, then asked for wisdom and faith to do whatever he wanted. Neither was sure how long the prayer lasted. But that didn't really matter. They continued praying, not wanting to stop until they were positive that the Lord had strengthened them. What was most important for them was to know whether God wanted them to go to the ceremony. At the conclusion of the prayer, both were certain.

They had to go.

~

The ceremony was in full swing when Becka and Scott arrived. A large fire burned in the center of the clearing. A dozen dancers, all dressed in colorful costumes with faces painted different colors, moved slowly around the fire to the beat of the ever present drums. Most of those gathered were barefoot.

Sara Thomas was nowhere to be seen.

Big Sweet, on the other hand, was. He wore the same battered straw hat he'd had on earlier and chewed on a piece of sugar-cane. He sat in a big wicker chair that looked more like a piece of run-down patio furniture than a seat of honor. Every once in a while, he smiled and waved at Becka and Scott from across the sea of dancers.

Finally the drumming stopped.

Big Sweet stood and chanted in a language Becka didn't understand. She guessed that it was probably French or Creole. At the end of what seemed to be a prayer, the drums began beating again— much faster this time.

Big Sweet raised his arms to the sky. "I call upon you, *Bon Dieu.*" He closed his eyes and waved his arms. "Bring forth the *loa* now to guide the people."

As soon as he returned to his chair, the drums churned out an even faster rhythm.

"I know *loa* means the dead," Becka whispered to Scott, "but who is *Bon Dieu* again?"

"I think he's the most powerful of the gods," Scott whispered back. "Kind of like the supreme ruler."

Most of the dancers moved in the same undulating rhythm as they had before. Others jerked spasmodically like puppets on a string. A few threw themselves to the ground, twitching like bugs in the dirt. One man ran wildly around the circle as fast as he could, screaming hysterically until he collapsed on the ground from exhaustion.

"This is getting too weird," Scott whispered.

Becka nodded. Once again she had a sick feeling in the pit of her stomach that they were in over their heads. But the prayers and the Bible verses they had read still echoed in her heart. She knew that they were exactly where they were called to be. Not only would God protect them, but he would also show them what to do.

On the other side of the dancers, she noticed a man whose face was painted bright red. She also noticed that he glared at them. She nudged her brother. "Do you see that man? The one with the red face?"

Scott looked around. "Nope. I see a green-faced man, a guy with orange spiders on his cheek, a woman with a blue star on her forehead, and . . . oh, that guy. What's the matter with him?"

Becka gulped. "He's coming over here."

Scott shook his head. "No, he's not. He's just heading out to . . . wait. He *is* coming over here."

The red-faced man never took his eyes off

Becka and Scott as he used his walking stick to clear the dancers out of his way. He towered over them. *"Sama sama tay, sama sama tay!"* he shouted, pointing at them.

A few of the dancers nearby stopped and stared at Becka and Scott.

Suddenly the red-faced man leaped high into the air and screamed, *"AIEEEEEEYA!"*

The cry sent chills through Becka. She glanced at Scott in a silent signal to hold their ground.

The drums stopped beating. Everyone quieted.

"Sama sama tay!" The red-faced man shouted, still pointing at Becka and Scott. *"Sama sama tay!"*

The whole group stared now. Becka tensed. She waited, silently praying. Others in the group joined in with the red-faced man, chanting, *"Sama sama tay! Sama sama tay!"* They crowded around Scott and Becka.

"Sama sama tay! Sama sama tay!"

More and more joined in, pushing themselves closer and closer.

"Sama sama tay! Sama sama tay!"

The red-faced man raised his walking stick high into the air.

"Sama sama tay! Sama sama tay! SAMA SAMA TAY! SAMA SAMA TAY!"

Becka wanted to bolt, to break through the

crowd. She was sure the red-faced man intended to crack either Scott or her over the head with his stick. But instead of running, she closed her eyes and prayed for all she was worth. She hoped Scott did the same.

Suddenly the conch horn sounded.

Everyone froze and turned toward Big Sweet. He blew the giant shell two more times.

The red-faced man was not about to give up. He pointed at Becka and Scott and shouted, *"Sama sama tay!"*

Big Sweet angrily shook his head. "No! No *sama sama tay. Untero tay. Untero my tay!"*

The dancers seemed relieved by what they heard and turned away. But the red-faced man still pointed at Becka and Scott.

"No!" Big Sweet shouted again. *"Untero tay! My tay!"*

The red-faced man stepped back. He gave a slight bow in Big Sweet's direction and rejoined the group. The drums began again, and the dancers resumed their gyrations.

"What was *that* all about?" Scott whispered.

"That fellow thought you were intruders—spies trying to steal our secrets," Big Sweet replied. "I told him you were my guests. Potential members to join the group."

"Potential members?!" Scott shouted, incredulously. "You told him that?!"

Big Sweet laughed. "Who knows? The night is young."

Before Scott could respond, a pale girl broke through the brush and entered the ring of dancers.

"Look." Scott pointed. "It's Sara."

Though she wore nothing unusual—just high school PE shorts and a T-shirt—Sara stood out dramatically from the dancers. True enough, most of the others were having some kind of experience. But Sara seemed to be fighting a war. She contorted one moment, flowed with the rhythm of the drums the next, then contorted again, fighting against something with all her strength.

Slowly Big Sweet stood. This time he shouted out the names of several spirits. Some he called *rada loas*.

The drummers increased their tempo. Big Sweet walked through the dancers until he finally arrived at Sara's side. "And you, Sara? Are you ready for your final rite of initiation into our group?"

Suddenly Sara stopped moving. She glared at Big Sweet and tried to shake her head. But her whole body began to tremble.

Scott leaned over to Becka and whispered, "Look at her eyes. She's scared to death! She's trying to fight this thing."

Scott was right. The girl's eyes were wild

and filled with fear as her body shook harder and harder, clearly out of control.

Becka rose to her feet. "We have to help her. We have to—"

Animal growls suddenly came from Sara's mouth. Her body twisted and contorted uncontrollably.

Big Sweet tried to embrace her, but she pushed him away and flung herself to the ground.

The crowd began to murmur, but Big Sweet raised his hands. "Sara is fighting with her *petro loa* for control of her body. She will tear herself apart unless I can quiet the spirit with the magic balm."

"No!" Becka called. She started to push her way through the crowd. "Don't—"

But her voice was drowned out as Sara began shrieking and rolling in the dirt. Big Sweet signaled two other men for help. It took all three of them to hold her.

"No!" Becka repeated. "She doesn't need potions! She needs—"

Sara's scream was unearthly, unrecognizable, as Big Sweet applied some special ointment. Then, almost instantly, she quieted. The fit subsided, and she lay perfectly still.

Scott and Becka stared.

"I guess he does have power," Scott finally ventured.

But Becka wasn't convinced. There was something wrong. She couldn't put her finger on it, but something wasn't right.

The drums began again, and the dancers resumed their actions. Big Sweet turned to Scott and smiled triumphantly. But Becka barely noticed. As she knelt beside Sara, she knew what was wrong.

Sara wasn't breathing.

Quickly Becka reached for Sara's neck, searching for a pulse. There was none.

"She's dead!" Becka cried. "Sara's dead!"

8

Immediately Becka and Scott put their CPR training to work. Scott blew air into Sara's mouth several times while Becka pumped Sara's chest.

"It's not working!" Becka shouted.

"We've gotta keep trying!" Scott yelled.

Becka continued pumping Sara's chest. But it was no use.

"Still no response!" Becka cried, feeling for Sara's pulse again. "We have to get her to the hospital."

Big Sweet offered his battered pickup truck. They quickly loaded Sara into the back. Becka and Scott crawled in with her to resume CPR as Big Sweet sped off.

"I've seen this before!" Big Sweet called through the back window. "When the *petro loa* gets violent, the magic balm sends the *loa cheval* into a deep sleep. She will wake up OK. I give you my word."

"She's dead!" Becka shouted. Her eyes burned with tears. "Don't you get it? She's dead!"

"Don't blame yourself!" Scott shouted over the wind. "We did everything we could do! Like Pastor Barchett said, you can't deliver someone if she doesn't want—"

"But she did!" Becka cried, wiping the tears out of her eyes. "She wanted to be delivered. I could see it in her eyes. She was fighting for control when that demon killed her!"

Minutes later Big Sweet skidded the pickup into the emergency entrance of Sorrento's hospital. Scott threw down the gate while Big Sweet scooped up Sara and raced inside with her.

An orderly helped him get her onto a gurney, while an admissions staff person asked questions in the background. Becka gave the admissions clerk all the information she knew as the orderly wheeled Sara into another room. Scott and Big Sweet stayed behind near the hospital entrance.

Time passed while the emergency room team worked on Sara. Becka paced in the narrow waiting area. She stopped as Scott approached. "Where's Big Sweet?" she asked.

Scott gave a slight shrug. "He had to get back to the ceremony."

"He what?!" Becka felt herself growing angry.

"Yeah, he said the people needed him and, uh . . ."

"And what?"

"And that . . . well . . . that Sara would be all right."

Becka couldn't believe what she heard. She slumped into a chair, feeling a sudden chill. Her fever was on the rise again. It drained what little energy she had left. She was angry, scared, and reaching the point of total exhaustion.

Scott sat beside her. "Are you gonna be OK?"

"I don't know." Once again hot tears sprang to her eyes. She tried to blink them back but couldn't. Finally she turned to

Scott. "Someone died, Scotty. That's never happened to us before."

Scott nodded.

"Where's all our power? All those verses said we're supposed to have the victory."

Scott looked away. When he spoke, his voice was thick and faint. "I don't know."

"I'm scared, Scotty."

"Don't say that," he said. "Fear is a weapon of the enemy. If we believe he has the power instead of God, then he can beat us."

"He's already beaten us."

"Don't say—"

"She's dead, Scott! We lost! She's dead!"

"Excuse me?"

They both looked up to see a nurse approach. She seemed nervous. "Are you the ones who brought Sara Thomas in?"

"Yes," Becka said, already preparing herself for the worst.

"Well . . ." The nurse took a breath. "She's gone."

Becka nodded. "I know. We were just hoping you could do something to—"

"No, you misunderstand me," the nurse said. "She's not gone as in dead. She's gone as in she left the hospital."

"She what?!"

"I don't know where she went. When she arrived in the ER, I checked her vital signs.

One minute I couldn't detect any, and the next . . . she just sat up and said she was fine."

"How's that possible?" Scott asked.

"I couldn't believe it myself. I raced to get the doctor. But when we got back to the room, she was . . . gone."

Becka and Scott exchanged glances.

~

For several minutes Sara stood outside the hospital—the same hospital where John Noey and Ronnie Fitzgerald fought for their lives.

She felt terrible for them . . . and for herself.

Her identity seemed to ebb away. *I've used the power of voodoo,* she thought. *Now I must serve its power.*

The irony almost made her laugh, but she knew she must not. The *petro loa* in her demanded her vigilance. If she let down her guard, even for a moment, it would take over again. And then what little was left of Sara Thomas would vanish.

Completely.

Big Sweet had been right. He had told her that she could not resist the *petro loa* on her own. If she tried to stand against the spirit, it would make her insane. It would take complete control of her—maybe even kill her.

She remembered other bits of information he had given her after one ceremony.

"Can you heal me of the *petro loa?*" she had asked hopefully.

Big Sweet had only shaken his head. "No, I cannot do that. But I can teach you how to stay healthy while you learn its ways."

"Learn its ways?" she had asked. "What do you mean?"

"The *loa* may leave you in time, Sara, but for now, you must learn to live with it. Learn when it is awake and when it sleeps. Learn what it requires of you. Then you will be able to use what is left for yourself."

"You're asking me to let the spirit rule so that it might let me have a little of my life back?" she had asked incredulously.

Big Sweet had nodded. "I know no other way. When my father studied with Marie Leveau, we knew a man who had been a *loa cheval* for forty years. In the daytime he was a wonderful man. He used to take me fishing. He often brought little candies to us kids. But my father warned us to stay away from him at night. That was when his *petro loa* came out. He was very violent then. It took five men to hold him down. But his life was not a total loss. He had his days."

Unable to think of this any longer, Sara turned from the hospital and headed down the street. She didn't care where she walked or for how long. She just had to get away.

The streets of Sorrento seemed barren as Sara wandered them. Soon she passed the old church near the library where she worked. Unable to explain her attraction to it, she came to a stop in front of the church, then turned and moved up the stairs. She hesitated before trying the door.

It was open.

It was eerie inside the church at this hour. It was lit only by a small lamp near the front and a few votive candles.

Sara took another step inside and suddenly began to feel very nauseous. Holding her stomach, she turned to go when she was suddenly startled by the presence of an elderly man kneeling in the back pew. He was thin, and his white hair caught the moonlight.

She hoped he wouldn't notice her. But suddenly he looked directly into her eyes.

"Sara?" the elderly man stammered. It was obvious he was as surprised as she was.

For an instant Sara was frozen with shock. Who was this man? How could he know her name? The nausea suddenly increased. She backed away toward the door.

The elderly man rose unsteadily to his feet. "I am Pastor Barchett. Just now I was praying for you. Please, won't you—?"

Sara spun around to the door. The nausea was worse. She had to get out. Still, something inside was crying, begging her to stay. With great effort, she forced herself to turn around and face the pastor.

"Help me . . . ," she cried. "Please . . . help—"

Suddenly her mouth slammed shut. She spun around, then ran for the door.

"Sara, please—"

She could barely hear him over the laughter filling her head—taunting laughter that was not hers. She felt herself moving outside and down the steps. There was no stopping now—the *loa* was in charge again.

And it was forcing her to return to the ceremony.

～

"I say we go back," Scott insisted.

"Scotty . . ."

"Listen." Becka's brother was up on his feet, pacing. "We've done everything the Bible said, right?"

"Well, yeah, but—"

"We've prayed and believed, right? Just like Z suggested, just like that pastor guy said."

"I know that, but . . ."

"But what?"

"Scotty, she nearly died."

"But she didn't. Come on, Beck, where's your faith?"

"My faith is . . ." Becka took a long, deep breath and slowly let it out. Her temperature was up again. She fought off the chills. "I'd like to go, Scotty. But I'm . . . I've got nothing left."

Her brother looked at her.

"I'm sorry." She shook her head and pulled in her legs to try to keep herself warm. "I'm wiped out. I'm . . . I'm sorry."

Scott looked at her for a long moment. But instead of making her feel guilty, he quietly knelt beside her. "You're right. I don't know what I was thinking. It's been rough on you—way rougher than on me."

"I'm sorry," she repeated. "I feel like a total failure. But I just don't even think I could . . ."

"That's OK. You just stay here."

Becka stared at him. "What?"

"You stay here at the hospital and call Mom and Aunt Myrna to pick you up."

"You're not going alone?"

He slowly rose. "Beck, we came here to do a job."

"You saw the power there. You know what can—"

"I know, I know. We've lost a few battles

with this one. But the war isn't over. Not yet."
He headed for the door.

"Scott—"

" 'If you believe, you will receive whatever you ask for in prayer.' Remember, Beck?"

She struggled to her feet. "I know that, but—"

He turned back to her one last time. "Give Mom and Aunt Myrna a call. Have them pick you up. And then the three of you can pray for me."

"Scotty?"

"Pray a lot."

"You can't go there by yoursel—"

But he was already out the door. It slid shut behind him.

Becka fell back in her seat, feeling frustrated and exhausted. She closed her eyes, trying to think what to do. Scott must not go back to the ceremony alone. And yet—

"Excuse me, are you Sara Thomas's friend?"

Becka opened her eyes to see a young doctor standing in front of her. She nodded.

"We'd taken a sample of Sara's blood and were running some tests . . ."

"Yes?"

"Her blood seems to contain trace amounts of a rare poison."

"Poison?"

"Yes—curare. It's from a tree that grows in South America. When you apply it externally like a salve on the skin, it sometimes renders the victim unconscious. It can slow down the heartbeat to where life signs are very hard to detect."

Becka could hardly believe what she heard. "You mean it makes you look like you're dead?"

"Yes. If it's applied externally in small amounts, its effects last less than an hour, which explains Sara's return to consciousness. Unfortunately, if it's taken internally, or if the subject receives too much over a short period of time, well . . ." He hesitated.

"Please, go ahead," Becka insisted.

"I don't know where your friend would have contact with something like this, but she should be careful. If she's exposed to it again too soon, it will kill her."

Becka stood stunned, her mind reeling. The first time, Sara had been lucky. But if she was heading back to the ceremony, and if Big Sweet applied the poison again . . .

"Listen, you look a little pale," the doctor said. "Maybe we should take your temperature and—"

Becka started for the door. Of course he was right. She felt terrible. But Sara's life was in danger. And if somebody didn't tell her, if somebody didn't warn Big Sweet and Scott . . .

"No, I'm fine," she lied. "Thank you."

"Are you sure?" the doctor called.

But Becka was already out the door. As the doctor's question followed her, she shook her head. She wasn't sure she had the strength to make it back to the ceremony. But she *was* sure of one thing. She had to try.

"Help me," she prayed as she headed down the street. "Please, Lord, give me the strength I need."

9

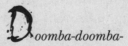oomba-doomba-
doom. Doomba-doomba-doom.

The drums echoed through the swamp.
Becka was fine as long as she could follow
their sound. The moon was three-quarters
full and bright enough to allow her to make
her way through the thick undergrowth.

She shivered, wondering if the cause was

her rising fever, the night air, or the resurgence of her fear. Probably all three.

Doomba-doomba-doom. Doomba-doomba-doom.

Somehow she managed to avoid falling into the water or running face first into branches—both strong possibilities when stumbling through the bayou at night.

Doomba-doomba-doom. Doomba-doomba-doom.

But she still had the drums to direct her. She still had—

Suddenly, they stopped.

Becka hesitated, straining to hear the slightest sound, the slightest clue. None was forthcoming. She had never been in this part of the swamp. Without the drums, she was lost.

Panic gripped her. She wanted to run, to scream for help, to plow through the swamp and its treacherous waters, to keep running and running—running to get out of the swamp, running to help her brother, running to prevent Big Sweet from reapplying his magic balm on Sara.

She struggled with fear—the same fear that had been her enemy throughout the trip. Fear on the plane, the fear of the thresher, and the fear of Sara's curse . . .

"No!" she shouted to no one in particular. "I am not afraid!"

The fear subsided but only for a moment.

"NO!" she repeated. But the fear left and returned even faster. So she did the only thing she could think of. She began quoting Bible verses—some she had learned as a child and some she had read with Scott earlier that evening.

" 'The Spirit who lives in you is greater than the spirit who lives in the world. . . . If you believe, you will receive whatever you ask for in prayer. . . . Perfect love expels all fear. . . .' " As she continued, the fear slowly faded. A peace settled over her. Filling her head with God's truth left no room for fear's lies.

As the peace came, so did a quiet logic. She decided to sit on a nearby log and wait patiently for the drums to resume.

But what if the drums never started again? What if the ceremony was over? What if Sara was already—

Once again Becka thought of the verses. Once again a gentle peace settled over her. Soon she could hear the soft rhythmic chirp of crickets. A thousand tiny insects buzzed. Frogs called from deep within the swamp. The place was a virtual symphony of nature.

Yes, God was good. Very good.

An owl hooted from a distant tree. She soon heard a splash as an animal entered the water, followed by the rattle of a snake. . . .

A snake! Becka froze.

Maybe she was wrong. Maybe it was something else.

No, there it was again. It was a snake's rattle. It was closer than before.

Becka peered at the ground around her feet, looking for some movement.

None came.

The rattle had seemed to come from the left side. She rose, preparing to run to the right.

Then she heard the rattle again.

This time it came from the right.

Ever so slowly, Becka turned. Out of the corner of her eye she saw it. Something slithered along the ground. She turned fast to the left.

Too fast.

Her foot caught on the log. As she toppled forward, she tried to shift but fell backward, arms flailing as she tried to regain her balance.

It did no good.

She landed exactly where she didn't want to be—less than a yard from the snake.

The rattler raised itself up, preparing to strike.

"Please, Jesus," she cried, "make it go away!"

As if in answer, the snake rattled even

more menacingly and reared its head back.
Becka could see its silver black eyes glaring at
her in the moonlight. She closed her eyes,
expecting the worst. Then, just as suddenly
as it had risen, the snake lowered itself to the
ground and slithered off in the opposite
direction.

Becka watched, amazed at how loudly her
heart was pounding. She realized that the
pounding she heard wasn't her heart, but
the drums.

She stood up, took a deep breath to steady
herself, and headed toward the sound.

~

Big Sweet nodded slightly when Scott
entered the clearing and found a place in
the outside circle. The dancers had already
worked themselves into a frenzy as they
chanted, whirled, sang, and screamed.

Immediately Scott spotted Sara. She
danced with the same jerky movements as
before, all the while crying out in a strange
language. Her voice was unnaturally deep
and husky.

Scott knew the signs.

Sara was possessed.

The time for action had come. He started
toward her.

The showdown was about to begin.

Big Sweet also rose from his wicker chair.
He wasn't sure what Scott was about to do,
but he wasn't taking any chances. The *petro
loa* in Sara Thomas was powerful. If it was
cast out of Sara, there was no telling how
many of his people it would attack. He would
not let them be injured.

Carefully he reached into the leather bag
hanging from the back of his chair. He
extracted a small tin container. In it was the
same potion he had used earlier that night—
a potion from the strychnos tree. The tree
was originally from South America. Big
Sweet's father had transplanted it in the
bayou when Big Sweet was a small boy. Its
resin was black and brittle. When mixed with
certain roots, it turned into a dark brown
salve. This was his magic balm.

Scott continued toward Sara. He was ten
feet away when she suddenly spun around.
She seemed to stare right through him.

Scott had seen that cold, lifeless stare
before. He knew that something else looked
through Sara's eyes. That something else was
what Big Sweet called the *petro loa*. Scott
knew it by another name. Demon.

He came to a stop. Slowly, he raised his
right hand. The battle was about to begin.

Sara moved like a puppet. She suddenly
snatched a walking stick from a nearby

dancer and twirled around, catching Scott off guard. She slammed the stick against Scott's knee, knocking him to the ground.

The demon caused Sara to lunge at him once more, then raised Sara's arm for another blow.

"No!" Big Sweet shouted. He held the open container in his left hand. The fingers of his right hand were covered with a white powder to shield him from the effects of the magic balm. "I speak to the *petro loa* occupying Sara Thomas. You shall not hurt this boy."

Sara's head nodded in agreement, but the nodding grew more rapid and exaggerated until it was obvious that the spirit mocked Big Sweet.

Scott raised himself to one knee, trying to clear his head. But instantly the *petro loa* swung the big stick down hard on his shoulder. He cried out in pain.

Big Sweet motioned to his men. Three of them leaped on Sara from behind while Big Sweet dug his hand into the tin of magic balm, preparing to smear it on her.

Sara struggled and almost broke free. A fourth man soon joined the fray. The four managed to hold her down. Big Sweet moved to smear the balm on her arm.

"Stop!" Becka ran into the clearing. "Don't touch her with that! It's poison!"

Big Sweet looked at her. "I must use the magic balm to quiet the *petro loa!*" he shouted. "It will not kill! It will make the *loa* sleep! You saw yourself!"

Becka strode quickly toward them. "It *will* kill!"

Big Sweet frowned.

Becka continued. "I spoke to a doctor at the hospital. He said the more you use it, the more dangerous it is. You've already used some to knock her unconscious. He said that if you use more too soon, it will kill her."

"But I must quiet the *petro loa* before he brings harm to her or to one of my people. Look at your brother."

"I'm OK," Scott said, struggling to his feet. "Nothing's broken."

Sara's body writhed once again. The four men struggled to hold her down.

Big Sweet started toward her once more. "I must quiet the *petro loa.*"

"*I* will quiet the *petro loa!*" Becka shouted.

All eyes turned to her. She nodded at Scott.

He slowly rose to his feet, returning her nod with a thumbs-up.

She took a deep breath. Turning to face Sara, Becka called out in a loud voice, "In the name of Jesus Christ of Nazareth, I command you to come out of her!"

Nothing happened.

Becka moved closer. "Demon who occupies Sara Thomas, you come out of her now, in the name of Jesus Christ! I order it!"

Suddenly, with superhuman strength, Sara tossed aside the four men who held her. She rose to face Becka. "Who are you?" Sara's mouth moved, but the voice was guttural. "Why do you force your will on others?"

"It doesn't matter who I am," Becka said with confidence. "I am not the one forcing my will. You are! Now, be gone in the name of Jesus Christ—"

"What makes you think—?"

Becka cut the demon's words short with a sharp motion of her hand. She knew all too well how demons argued only to stall or weaken a believer's faith. She would allow neither. She couldn't afford to. "I said go in the name of Jesus Christ! Now!"

Sara's body tensed as if charged by electricity. She let out a loud, ghastly cry before dropping to the ground.

All who watched gasped. Many began to murmur, wondering at the power they had just witnessed.

Becka moved to kneel beside the still girl and tenderly touched her arm. "Sara," she said. "Sara, it's OK now. Sara . . ."

Sara's eyes snapped open. Before Becka

could move, the girl kicked her with all her might.

Becka cried out, tumbling backward.

"There's more than one of them!" Scott yelled.

Sara leaped to her feet and started for Becka.

"Stop!" Scott shouted. "Enough trickery! I command you to stop in the name of Jesus!"

Sara froze, then slowly faced him with a look of menace.

Faith surged through Scott. He was not about to be intimidated, not when he knew who truly held the power in this situation. "We command you in the name of Jesus Christ to be gone! We cast you into the pit!"

Becka struggled back to her feet and approached from the other side. "Be gone. All of you! We cast all of you out of Sara and into the lake of fire. In the name of Jesus Christ, go!"

Sara's body began to tremble, her face contorting grotesquely. The onlookers backed away. Some turned and ran.

Sara threw her head back and shrieked a long, agonizing wail, more animal than human. It echoed through the trees and across the swamp. Finally, she collapsed on the ground, unconscious.

Becka and Scott looked at each other. They knew she was clean this time. All of the demons had gone. They knelt beside Sara.

"Sara?" Becka said. "Sara?"

A moment later, the girl's eyelids flickered, then opened fully.

"Are you all right?" Becka asked.

Sara nodded. "I think . . ." Her voice was hoarse. She licked painfully dry lips. Her eyes looked weary but hopeful. "The spirit's gone, isn't it?"

Becka nodded. "Yes." She started to add, "All of them are" but changed her mind.

Relief crossed Sara's face. For the first time she seemed to relax.

"Is this what you want?" Becka asked. "To be totally free of that kind of spirit forever?"

Sara nodded. "Yes . . . yes . . . of course." Then her forehead wrinkled. "But what about . . . what I did to John and Ronnie?"

"Are you sorry you hurt them?" Scott asked.

"Yes." There was no mistaking the sadness in Sara's voice. "I am very sorry."

Becka smiled warmly. "Then why don't you pray for them with us?"

"Pray? To who?"

"To the very person who gave us the power to cast out the *petro loa*," Scott answered her.

Sara looked at him. Slowly she nodded.

Becka and Scott bowed their heads. After a moment, Sara followed suit.

"Dear Jesus," Becka began, "we ask your forgiveness for what Sara has done."

"Forgive me," Sara murmured. "And forgive me for what I did to Becka . . . by trying to put a curse on her. I'm so sorry for that!"

Becka sighed. "I also forgive her for that, Lord. And we ask that you heal those boys. Make them whole again."

Sara nodded, tears forming in her eyes.

"And, Lord," Becka continued, "please reveal your love to Sara. Help her know your truth."

Sara began to sob.

Becka prayed silently for several moments. When she finished, she looked up at Big Sweet. He seemed astonished by the encounter with the demon and the prayer that followed.

"The magic balm is dangerous," she said.

Big Sweet nodded. "I will not use it again. I only did as my father taught me. The *petro loa* was bad."

"It was a demon," Scott explained. "Not the spirit of someone who died but a fallen angel. A demon—more than one, actually."

Big Sweet sighed. "Perhaps."

"We believe in one God," Becka explained, "the *Bon Dieu* who rules over everything."

"*Bon Dieu.*" Big Sweet nodded in agreement. "That I understand. But he does not communicate with us."

"He does through his Son," Becka said. "And it was the power of his Son that you saw demonstrated here tonight."

Big Sweet met her eyes. "His Son?"

"That's right," Becka said. "Jesus."

10

 ecka and Scott
invited Sara back to Aunt Myrna's that night.
The three of them talked long into the early
hours of the morning.

"I'm really sorry for the way I treated you,"
Sara said. "I—I was just afraid, after what I
did to John and Ronnie, that somebody
would try to . . ." She dropped off, then

shook her head and resumed. "It seems funny now, but this last week it's like all these things happened to someone else. Like it wasn't even me."

"In a way it wasn't," Becka explained. "The more you got involved with voodoo, the more you lost yourself."

Sara shuddered at the thought. "I'm just glad it's finally over."

Becka and Scott exchanged looks.

"Actually—" Scott cleared his throat—"it isn't over . . . at least not yet. But it can be."

Sara looked up concerned. "What do you mean?"

"Those evil spirits—they'll try to come back."

Sara sank deeper into the chair. "Oh, no!"

Scott nodded. "The Bible says they will come back if you haven't filled up the vacancy they left."

"Filled the vacancy?" Sara asked.

Becka explained. "The only thing that can protect you from evil spirits is accepting Jesus Christ as your Lord and Savior. Once that happens, once he's in your heart, then when they try to return, you'll have the authority to stop them."

"Are you serious?" Sara asked. "I can have that authority?"

Becka and Scott nodded.

"Well, what do I have to do?"

Carefully Becka and Scott explained how Jesus died on the cross to forgive Sara of her sins. They told her about his being raised from the dead. All she had to do was ask him to forgive her, since he already took the punishment for those sins.

"That's it?" Sara asked.

"That's only half," Scott said. "You also need to let him be your Lord."

"Lord?"

"Yeah, you know—like your boss. The boss of your whole life."

"You mean let him be the boss instead of me?"

Scott nodded. "No offense, but so far things haven't turned out so great with you in charge." He groaned at Becka's quick nudge to his ribs.

Sara nodded, almost smiling. "Then that's what I want to do," she said. "I want to give your Jesus all of my life. I've had lots of trouble. I don't want any more."

"It isn't so much that you won't have trouble," Becka corrected. "It's just that Jesus will always be there to show you the way through any troubles you encounter."

Tears welled up in Sara's eyes. "That's really all I've ever wanted—somebody to show me the way."

And so, after they were sure that Sara understood and was serious about her decision, Becka and Scott led her in prayer. Together they helped her ask Jesus to forgive her of her sins and to come into her heart as the Lord of her life. Soon, before they even knew it, all three were crying and hugging one another. They knew it was just the beginning. Sara would still have a lot to deal with. But she no longer faced the battle on her own.

It was nearly sunrise when Aunt Myrna agreed to drive Sara home. And after several good-byes and a few more hugs, Becka and Scott headed back into the house to get some sleep.

"Can you believe it?" Becka asked. "Everything worked out."

"It sure did," Scott replied. "Not the way we thought it would, but better."

"That's the weird thing about God," Becka said. "He never does things our way."

"Guess he just wants it done right." Scott smirked.

"Guess so."

Becka was asleep before her head hit the pillow. This time, there were no dreams, no tossing and turning—just sleep. Deep, peaceful sleep—something she had needed for days; something she finally enjoyed.

The next day flew by. Before long, Becka, Scott, and Mom were packed and riding in the car back to the airport.

"Where're you going, Aunt Myrna?" Becka asked as the car pulled onto the main road and turned left instead of right. "This is the way to Sorrento, not the airport."

"Oh, I know, honey, but I wanted to show you something."

Minutes later they passed the library and pulled up in front of Pastor Barchett's church.

"What's going on?" Scott asked.

"Just hold on," Mom said. "You'll see."

They climbed out of the car and headed up the steps to the door.

"Good," Aunt Myrna said, looking inside. "We're just in time." She opened the door wider. They all slipped into the church.

Only a handful of people occupied the church. But there, standing up front in the baptistry, were Pastor Barchett and Sara Thomas.

Pastor Barchett was in the middle of speaking. "And do you, uh . . ."

"Sara," she quietly reminded him.

"Yes, of course." He cleared his throat. "And do you . . . Sara, fully understand what you are about to do?"

Sara nodded, looking very solemn.

Becka and Scott watched in silent anticipation.

"Then—" the old man folded her arms in front of her—"I baptize thee in the name of the Father, and of Jesus Christ the Son, and of the Holy Spirit."

He lowered Sara back into the water, then lifted her again. She came out of the water looking radiant. Tears of joy mingled with the water streaming down her face.

Becka and Scott joined the others in applauding. But there was another sound— big, booming laughter, laughter that could only belong to . . .

Becka spun around. "Big Sweet! What are you doing here?" She smiled at the two little girls with him.

Big Sweet laughed again. "Why do you say that, Rebecca? I only tried to help Sara. I never wanted her to have such trouble."

Becka nodded. "You're right. I know that now."

He pulled his two daughters closer and continued. "My father taught me voodoo so I could protect myself and my family from bad spirits and curses. Sometimes it works—" he shrugged—"sometimes it doesn't. But this Jesus, this Son of *Bon Dieu,* the God of gods, has much power. I will come by this church

now and again to see what I see. What do you
think about that?"

"I think that's great," Becka said.

"Me, too," Scott agreed.

"I just have one question." It was Aunt
Myrna. "What about my goat?"

"I am sorry, Miss Myrna. It wandered onto
my place and joined the others. I did not
know it was yours. I will give you one of mine.
I will give you two."

Everyone applauded that decision.

Outside, the good-byes were brief.

"Come on," Mom fretted, "the plane won't
wait."

"Did you hear the news?" Sara asked. "John
Noey came out of his coma last night. And
they think Ronnie Fitzgerald will be OK,
too."

"That's great," Becka said.

"Looks like you got your first prayer
answered," Scott said to Sara.

She beamed. "And your aunt has hired me
to help her out a couple days a week."

"Well . . ." Aunt Myrna cleared her throat,
a little embarrassed. "I can use a good worker
like you around the house. Besides, I could
stand a little company, now that my family is
going."

"Oh, Aunt Myrna . . . ," Becka, Mom, and
Scott said together.

There was another round of hugs and more than a couple of tears as everyone congratulated Sara and said good-bye.

Then, just before Becka entered the car, Sara whispered something in her ear—something Becka would remember for as long as she lived. "Thank you for showing me the real power," she whispered as she gave her a final hug, "and the real love."

~

Becka's heart leaped to her throat as she saw Ryan Riordan waiting for them at the airport's baggage claim. He still had that incredible black hair, warm blue eyes, and of course, that killer smile.

"Ryan!" Before she knew it, she had thrown her arms around him.

"I really missed you," he said, pulling her back to look at her. His smile flashed again.

"I missed you, too."

"What about me?" Scott broke in. "Anybody miss me?"

Ryan scratched his head. "Dunno, kid. That's a tough one. I'll let you know if I come up with someone."

Scott laughed. "I'll bet Cornelius did." Cornelius was the family's parrot. "That poor bird is probably tired of having only Darryl to squawk at for nearly a week." Darryl was his best friend. "Maybe Darryl's tired of being squawked at too!"

The rest of the group laughed and agreed.

It was just like old times as the good-natured bantering began. But later that evening, when Ryan joined them at home and asked Becka to take a short walk with him, his mood had changed considerably.

"Beck, I've been waiting till we were alone to ask you something."

Becka caught her breath, hoping for some heartfelt words of romance. But when she saw the look in Ryan's eyes, she knew he had something else in mind besides romance.

"I really worried about you while you were away. Is this going to be, like, a regular thing . . . you running off to some faraway place whenever that Z guy contacts you?"

"Of course not!" She laughed in relief. "We haven't heard from Z for a while. I'm sure this was just a onetime thing."

The tension left Ryan's face. Once again he broke into his killer smile. "That's good because I—"

"Hey, Beck!" Scott ran out of the house.

Oh, great, Becka thought, not at all pleased with her brother's timing.

"There's a message from Z on the computer. He has another assignment."

Her stomach tightened. "What?"

"Yeah, and here's what's really weird. He wants you to go without me."

"Without you?" Becka asked. "Why? Where?"

Scott paused, purely—Becka was sure—for dramatic effect.

"Where?" she repeated impatiently.

He grinned and waggled his eyebrows. "Transylvania."

"Transylvania?" Becka was shocked. "Isn't that where all those stories take place . . . you know about . . . well, you know . . . ?"

"Vampires?" Scott said, grinning.

"But vampires don't . . ." Her voice trailed off.

"Exist?" Scott asked.

Becka nodded numbly.

Scott shrugged. "According to Z, something over there has got some actress scared out of her wits. He wants you to check it out."

Becka turned to Ryan, unsure what to say.

But as always, he made it easy. "It's all right, Beck. . . . I understand."

"Oh, and something else," Scott said.

They both turned back to him.

"He'll send a ticket for Ryan, too!"

Becka and Ryan stared at each other. Ryan raised his eyebrows.

"In the mood for a vacation?" Becka asked meekly.

Ryan tried to smile. "Sure, why not?"

But she was sure he was thinking the same thing she was . . . Transylvania? *Vampires* . . . ?

What was Z getting them into now?

AUTHOR'S NOTE

As I developed this series, I had two equal
and opposing concerns. First, I didn't want
the reader to be too frightened of the devil.
Compared to Jesus Christ, Satan is a wimp.
The two aren't even in the same league.
Although the supernatural evil in these
books is based on a certain amount of fact,
it's important to understand the awesome
protection Jesus Christ offers to all who have
committed their lives to him.

This brings me to my second and some-
what opposing concern: Although the powers of darkness are nothing compared to the
power of Jesus Christ and the authority he
has given his followers, spiritual warfare is
not something we casually stroll into. The situations in these novels are extreme to create
suspense and drama. But if you should find
yourself involved in something even vaguely
similar, don't confront it alone. Find an
older, more mature Christian (such as a par-
ent, pastor, or youth leader) to talk to. Let
them check the situation out to see what is
happening, and ask them to help you deal
with it.

Yes, we have the victory through Christ,
but we should never send in inexperienced
soldiers to fight the battle.

Oh, and one final note. When this series was conceived, there were really no bad guys on the Internet. Unfortunately that has changed. Today there are plenty of people out there trying to draw young folks into dangerous situations through it. Although the characters in this series trust Z, if you should run into a similar situation, be smart. Anyone can *sound* kind and understanding, but their intentions may be entirely different. All that to say, don't take candy from strangers you see . . . or trust those you don't.

Bill

FORBIDDEN ● DOORS

Want to learn more?

Visit Forbiddendoors.com on-line for
special features like:
- a really cool movie
- post your own reviews
- info on each story and its
  characters
- and much more!

Plus—Bill Myers answers your questions!
E-mail your questions to the author. Some
will get posted—all will be answered by
Bill Myers.

WheRe
AdvEnture
beGins
with
a BoOk!

LoG oN @
Cool2Read.com